STATES OF GRACE

STATES OF GRACE

Stories

STEPHEN GRAHAM JONES

"Bestiary" originally published in *Yellow Medicine Review*, Spring 2007.

"The Boy Who Cried About Werewolves" originally published in *Critically Acclaimed: Fake Movies, Real Reviews*, ed. by Adam Cushman. Rare Bird Books, 2018.

"How to Know You're a Killer" originally published in *The Big Click*, Jul. 2014.

"The Joneses" originally published in *Air/Light*, Summer 2022.

"The Lepidopterists" originally published in *Cutbank*, Summer/Autumn 2023.

"The Real Batman Story" originally published as "Bats" in *Automata Review*, Jun. 2018.

"So This Is What It's Like" originally published in *F(r)iction*, Dec. 2020.

"Truth Is a Bearded Lady" originally published in *Microfiction Monday*, Jun. 2, 2014.

"The Umbrella Tree" originally published in *Texas Highways*, Aug. 2023.

"Why I Write" originally published in *Yellow Medicine Review*, Spring 2021.

ISBN: 979-8-3372-0094-1

This edition published in 2025 by Open Road Integrated Media, Inc.
180 Maiden Lane
New York, NY 10038
www.openroadmedia.com

CONTENTS

CONTENTS

CONTENTS

917 WORDS BEFORE WE BEGIN

I'll never not be in love with flash fiction. Or call it sudden fiction, like the book that changed so many of us. Some of these were published as prose poetry, which was weird to me, but sure, why not. It's an honor. Remember when *Esquire* used to close each issue with "Snap Fiction"? I miss those days. Lydia Davis was making flash a viable option, just by doing it at such a high level, poets were writing amazing paragraph-story things, I'm not sure what to call them except "beautiful," and everywhere you looked there was another flash fiction contest, or call, or opportunity.

In grad school at Florida State University, when *Sun Dog* was becoming *The Southeast Review*, I was a reader—"judge" is too lofty a word, as I was more a slushpile reader—for The World's Best Short-Short Story Contest, which is a mouthful, now that I search it up to get it right. To us it was always the "Best Short-Short Contest," but I don't recall any of us ever weaponizing that for a chuckle. We were so intent on finding gold in this slushpile, I mean. And did we ever. After that I fell into a whole string of other judging situations, from sites to magazines to national-level stuff, but I've stopped doing that these last few years—I realized I was just chasing that initial hopefulness of finding the perfect, immaculate story told in five hundred words.

There's a magic in that.

If I could make a living writing only flash fiction? I might do that. It's forever my favorite mode—and I do submit that that's what it is, as what it does is too motile and energetic to ever be captured under the umbrella of genre, which is about repeat-able conventions and formulae. Try to catch flash fiction under the pad of your index finger, though, and it slips away, turns into a recipe that's got a story there between the ingredients. But make whatever dish that's instructions for, and you end slipping a piece of your life into that casserole dish, and having to look away to keep your eyes from spilling down onto this paper you don't want to mess up, since it needs sharing, now that you see what's going on.

The stories in here, I can't really put a range of dates on them. Well, okay: maybe . . . 1996 or 1997 through . . . a month or two ago, here in January 2025? I'm still writing flash, yes. I can't help writing flash. I can't stop writing flash. But I did used to write a lot more flash. Until standing up at the mic of an auditorium reading some of these to people—flash is the fiction that goes over best out-loud, as you can really hear the joke-structure of storytelling laid bare—I never realized that so many of these small stories were written when my kids were under six or seven years old. Those are the years I call the Bounty Select-a-Size years: there was always something to dab up. I always had a half-size paper towel in my hand, was just following those two kids from this mess to that spill to the next disastrophe.

Thing was, sometimes I'd just collapse into a corner and watch them.

And I had a pull of paper towel there in my hand.

It's where so many of the stories here in *States of Grace* were scribbled down. So I want to say that I wrote them because I'm so compelled by some great eternal love affair with flash fiction. But be honest, Steve: it's because the lower-right corner of the sort-of page all these stories were happening on was always coming fast, so I had to start wrapping things up even faster. Under that kind of pressure to end, the story writhes and opens in new ways. It's like you've poured tears into a kaleidoscope, along with more than a little blood, and you're just finding out that that's not plastic flecks down against that glass, it's not the aquarium gravel it looks like. It's Pop-Rocks, isn't it? No, that's just what it looks like too: what it is is *larvae*—which is the second time in this little show intro-thing I've used that weird Latinate plural, isn't it? And, look: did I just also say "*Latinate*"?

I must be nervous, trying to be some writer I'm not, and never was.

Words are weird, aren't they?

Weird but wonderful.

But, yes, I am nervous. What if when I wrote the fifty stories in the original *States of Grace*, I was a different writer? What if I had some magic then that I don't have now, and never will again? What if I'm just reaching? What if what I'm getting down onto the page now in short-short form has lost some essential essence? If one of these new pieces were in the new *Sun Dog*'s slushpile, would it even make it into the second round?

I don't know.

You never do, with writing.

But you send it out, see, don't you?

That's what this is, for me.

Until then, I'll be here in my head like I always am, lying on my back and not aiming a telescope up at the sun to burn a hole in the back of my eye, but a kaleidoscope, one filled with all my hopes and fears, my memories and regrets.

They're all melting together again.

Look.

Stephen Graham Jones
31 January 2025
Boulder, Colorado

DEDICATION

This is to Tammy Carlton, who sat two seats up and one over in fourth grade, and said once "Why don't you just write a book about it?" This during my explanation to the teacher about the gum and monkey bars thing. This is to Ms. Glynnis from my sixth grade science, for reading my note out loud to the class in a voice I still hear. This is to Michael K. and Lacy and Nicholas, for paying for their order at my drive-through window that time with a squirrel scraped up from the street. This is especially to Lacy, for looking at me like she regretted that these kinds of things had to happen. This is to my dad, too, of course. I really thought you were dead that one morning. And this is to Coach Barker, for throwing the ball just far enough that I had to cradle my arms out over the track that time. This is to Wayne and Wayne, for showing me that place behind the gym, between the air conditioner and the fence with all the newspapers blown up against it. It was perfect. This is to Tammy Carlton, for having to look away when I walked into senior prom. This is to her friends, all suddenly applying lipstick, their mouths definitely not laughing. This is to the band that night, for only playing slow songs. This is to the radio all these years later, for reminding me about those songs when I least expect it. This is to Wayne and Wayne, for slipping me a beer through the drive-through window once. This is to Albert, my assistant manager, for pretending not to see. This is to Albert, for having been seventeen once as well, I guess. This is to my step-mom, for threading my greasy bangs behind my ear in fifth grade, studying me, telling me I didn't really look like my dad at all, did I? This is to Officer P—, for understanding, once. Just letting me come home instead. This is to the swings that used to be down by the Western Auto, left over from some drive-in I'd never seen. This is to Debra G., for sitting with me on them that time, talking about everybody she hated, everything she was going to do someday. How it was all going to be different. This is to those guys I never knew from Permian, too. I probably had it coming. This is to my older brother Hector, for telling them that. This is to Michael K., for telling me Hector'd said that. This is to my dad, for taking me by the chin, looking at each side of my face, and nodding, not saying anything. This is to Albert, for asking who they were, then taking his apron off, stepping out onto the patio for a cigarette. This is to Nicholas, for joining the Army two months after Lacy turned up pregnant. This is to Mr. Reise, for pairing me up with her for lab, because she couldn't touch any chemicals. This is to Michael K., for calling out to us that there wasn't womb for us both at the table. This is to Tammy Carlton, for shrieking when I ran to the back of the room that day, for Michael K. This is to my step-mom again, for picking me up from the principal's office for fighting, and delivering me to my dad's work. This is to my dad, for asking me if I got any good licks in this time, or if I just laid there again. This is to the spiral notebook I used to carry, that everybody was dead in. This is to Ms. Glynnis, for intercepting the note I'd been sending across to Wayne in sixth grade, before I really knew him, asking if I could listen to his Queen cassette at lunch. This is to my locker, for hiding my face all those times between classes. And this is to Tammy Carlton still, for planting that gum on the monkey bars, that strung down into my hair, my shirt, so I had to wear something from the lost and found, so the teacher had to use scissors on the gum. And this is to my real mom, for not flashing down from the sky that day, her spike heels deep in the neck of that teacher, her hand smoothing my hair down like should happen, and this is to my dad, for keeping those high-heeled shoes in the first place, making his new wife wear them, never letting me tell, so that all the words and lies built up and built up, had to come out somewhere, someday. Now turn the page, start the story.

As in the real world, a fine line divides the perception of tran-
scendence in all things and a hedonistic obsession with their
surfaces.

—John N. Ganim

IN THE BEGINNING

Ask and you shall receive, she said to me in the back seat of my Dodge Rambler, parked at the end of the old airstrip we all knew about, my tires pulled right up to the edge of the crumbling asphalt, then leaned over the front seat just far enough to tune Tulsa in on the radio, just far enough that I could see the fig leaf tattooed into the base of her back, and then I drew her down to me and we closed our eyes to the cattle nosing our windows, waiting to be named, and it was good.

LUNCH

The girl I trade jokes with at the cafeteria I eat at on Mondays has a new one for me this time: her son is going to live with his grandmother for a while. I ask her why—we're laughing, in our way, her filling tea glasses (tea first, halfway up, then the ice, which I guess is something you learn), me sliding two pieces of pie onto one saucer, like they let me do—and she says she's sending him to her mother's because this morning when she went in to wake him for school his breath was white, because she doesn't have a heater in her house. But her mother does, one of those big ones that shoots heat up through a vent in the living room. And then she nods for me to take my pie, that it's okay.

At one point a few minutes later, eating whatever I'm eating, I see a guy about twenty-five stand up from his table, then pull his dad—I think it's his dad, anyway, but it could be a boss, I guess—but what the guy does is pull him up from his plate and arrange him into the very specific shape he needs him to be in, to properly show this complicated karate move he saw on a show last night, or just thought of, maybe.

Either way, his face when he slow-motions through the move is deadly serious, and he does the sound effects too, or holds his lips like he's making the sounds, and I look away, want to fall in love with something, the first thing I see, but close my eyes instead, know that next week, and the week after, I'll be eating in a different place.

MODERN LOVE

1.) My son's first-grade teacher doesn't shoot heroin anymore. If her pupils are dilated now, she says, it's with wonder. The children are supposed to have infected her with it. Maybe, I don't know. At dinner, anyway, my son wears long sleeves, to cover the ball-point pen track marks they all do to be like her. His breath through the baby monitor just five years ago is still so clear to me.

2.) Once when it was Paint-Your-Baby day at the stadium I hid him in blankets and smuggled him to the park. I'd meant for us to sit on the grass and make talking sounds, but instead just stood, clutching him, watching four women with a tarp stretched between them, taut as a trampoline. Every few seconds a straw man would rise up limp from the tarp, hang midair for a few impossible seconds, then fall, smiling the whole time. There was a rhythm to it I couldn't deny. It was my son's first sunburn.

3.) My father was the kind of physicist who, in his later years, wore his oxygen tank on his back when he came to visit. As if he was scuba-diving, just visiting from some higher

place. Like this place would kill him if he were to accidentally breathe it in. In the science he taught my son, people
didn't die, couldn't. His world was gluons and leptons and
Anafranil in controlled doses, when necessary.

4.) In the garage last week I found a letter my wife wrote to my
son when she was fifteen. She's thirty-four now. The letter
starts out "Dear Robert: Today the man who would have
been your father died in a stock tank. He was the first one
to dive in. It was beautiful. What can I tell you other than
that he couldn't imagine breaking the surface of the water
with anything other than his body?" The thing is, my son
is named Robert. And my father was named Robert. It all
seemed so natural a few days ago.

5.) Picture this: a man sits in a bar after his father's funeral, and
though he's hunched protectively over his beer, still, the fight
raging around him slings a dollop of blood into his mug.
The afterimage of the red arc lingers in the mirror longer
than nature should allow. The man follows it down to his
beer, now with blood blooming in it upside down. He looks
from side to side, for who might be watching, and, when no
one is, swirls his mug gently, keeps drinking.

6.) The most terrifying moment of the twentieth century has to
have been when I walked into the living room one night and
sat beside my wife in front of the TV. We watched it together
for a while and I didn't tell her that my love was like a wooly
mammoth frozen beneath the tundra, a half-chewed daisy
in its teeth, and she didn't tell me what I wanted to hear,
that topiary gardeners dream of a naturally occurring shrub
in the form of a horse. Instead I asked her if this was a

commercial we were watching, and she shrugged, and we waited it out.

7.) A strange attractor in a system of repetitive motion is a point which seems to be organizing the system when, in fact, it's the product of the organization itself. Which is an excuse, I know. But picture this: a woman's finger resting on the plunger of her cherished syringe. One day she pushes it down out of habit and forces me up through the green surface of the water, into another world. The grocery store, up one aisle and down another, until I slow at the perfume aisle. There's the policewoman who patrols my son's school. Who keeps him safe. She's trying on scents, as if any of them go with polyester. I fall so in love with her.

THE COMPLETE ABSENCE OF CATS IS ANOTHER DEFINITION FOR SILENCE

The tornado of my fourteenth year did many things. It placed Mrs. Zimmer's station wagon in Kim Stanley's lawn upside down, the antenna planted up to the base. It carefully took out each window on the east side of twelfth, even the stained glass of the church. It lifted every dry good in the grocery store and then held them up for nine impossible seconds, the metal shelving sighing a relief known only to Randy Wall, locked out of the stockroom by the older bagboys: not an egg was broken.

It worked a red-striped straw into the sticky black grain of the telephone pole in front of the bank. Until the straw rotted, it was a novelty to pretend you were drinking from it, let the warmth of the flashbulb—the fact that you were alive—wash over you. All but two of the seniors that year had their graduation pictures taken there. The other two had their diplomas handed over to their mothers. There was no eye contact. There was nothing to say. But that was all months ahead.

Right then it was still the wig store in the sky, and a clean, unlikely path around the junkyard, and the Luthers' Great Dane riding across town on a cushion of air, and Mrs. Zimmer with her face pressed to the headliner of her station wagon, her husband's bare legs approaching from the front door of Kim Stanley's house, his lunch hour. He tried to explain: it was an act of God. There wasn't a cat anywhere in the world.

All the bare mannequin heads from the wig store were never recovered, either. You can still find them in ditches with grass growing across their plastic scalps, and in chimneys, their eyes black and knowing, and falling from the sky, their lips composed, cheeks drawn in, about to smile, Rudolph the Great Dane watching them, waiting for them, his great tail fanning the grass slowly. He doesn't remember the Luthers at all, is an Allen dog now. But the straw. Pictures of it are in the display case in the court house—pictures of all of it, really, except me, and the lit cigarette the tornado had wedged between my fingers, and my father touching down directly across from me, his hair still airborne.

We stared at each other as the stained glass fell in slivers all around us and I held the smoke in deep deep, and then he said it—*I'll pretend I didn't see that*—and turned around, started picking through the rubble to what was left of our house, our town, our lives. Behind him I smiled, took one long, last drag, and then aimed it back out at the heavens, in thanks.

ANOTHER NIGHT, ANOTHER DEATH

I accidentally inhaled a full breath of candle smoke when I was blowing out a candle out I didn't even light in the first place. Do I have wax in my lungs now? What about when it hardens? Is this how Steve McQueen died? Should I go to the emergency room now or in the morning? Maybe antacids will help. And cough syrup. Though I need to look up if they interact. Is it too late to call someone? I probably should stay awake a few hours to be sure I don't die in my sleep. Surely I would have heard about this if it was a thing. Back when candles were the main light source, I bet a lot of idols breathed in just like I did, and were too close as well, so sucked in that oily smoke, died in their sleep. Is that why the mortality rate used to be so young? I can feel the wax hardening already. In the autopsy's blood report or whatever, there'll probably just be cough syrup and antacid, but that won't be the whole story. I should write a note in case the pathologist doesn't see the need to carve any deeper. It wasn't the meds, doc. It was the candle. And I wasn't even the one who lit it! I was just trying to keep the house from burning down, but because I grew up with light bulbs, am not the right kind of familiar with flames and smoke, now I'm coughing and strug-gling. I should call someone. I should stay awake. I'll leave the candle right by my bed, so the guilty party will be there when I'm found. Goodnight, world. I didn't think this was how it would and, but, like the candle, I flickered, I sputtered, and then all that was left was a toxic black ribbon, already erasing itself.

THE PIANO THIEF

It'll take him all of a month, longer if he's in love. But always at least those thirty days. Because a piano is heavy. What he's learned to do over the years, though, is take them piece by precious piece. The day before it starts, he might be your blind piano tuner, the one you usher in because he's just like on all the shows you've ever seen, his dog swishing its tail by the stool while he works his arcane magic. But that night when he comes back, his fingers retracing the security code he wasn't supposed to be able to see, there will be no dog. Just cat feet, padding across your foyer, stepping over and over into a hooded pool of light. He'll carry no bag, either, won't need one, as all he takes that first night alone is a single hammer, from a key not often used. The next night, however, if he can't help himself, he might be trying to balance a whole armful, the razor strings slung all over his body. Then, finally, three weeks into it maybe, the piano will be hollowed out, will have become a bed he can't help curling up in while you sleep, unaware of the man in your living room. And, if he's in love, and he usually is—why else take this kind of chance?—he might even oversleep, spend the day listening to the sounds of your house as it bustles and thrums, his face in that soundless dark place a listening grin. Soaking into the joists and dovetails and master carpentry all around him, threatening to deliver him down to the floor all at once, is a solvent he's developed over half a lifetime, derived from margarine and spray lubricant and a certain brand of hair tonic. What it does is loosen the fittings, allow the piano to whisper apart in the night, as if folding itself into nothing.

Which, for all intents and purposes, you'll think may just be the case. Provided you even notice the absence, after he's taken care to wirebrush the indentations out of the carpet and rearrange the furniture ever so slightly, so as to cover the glaring absence, the proof he was ever there. And, even when you do notice, of course it will be coincidence, bad luck—you could never in good conscience cast suspicion on the blind man with the good ear, now assembling your piano in one of the great empty rooms of his mansion across town. Not for the sound it can produce when tuned right and played better, either, but for the sound he was in love with—the sound *around* the piano, of a home, of people eating dinner, of baths starting and stopping, seemingly without reason or rhythm, but with a forward motion he can almost remember, a feeling that this is never going to end. Some nights, lying again in the casket he's so delicately reassembled, the wires finally still all around him, he'll be able to hear that forward motion again, even, that life, and he'll smile in the musty darkness, manage to forget for a few moments that the piano isn't his.

THE REAL BATMAN STORY

A boy on the cusp of puberty walks out of a theater with his parents one night, and a mugger's waiting in the alley for them. He only wants money and jewels, but, because this particular mugger has a gun, he takes more.

An orphan now, this morose boy retreats to his family estate away from the city and its now-obvious dangers, and the family butler does his best to give the boy room to grieve, space to grow. Taking a break from the studies and training that are supposed to eventually explain why what happened to his parents had to happen—the world no longer makes sense—the boy takes one of his rambling walks around the property. Not really going anywhere, just putting one foot after the other, and running through the paces of that night again: What he could have done different. What he *should* have done.

Because he's not paying attention, the boy wanders onto the rocky slope he'd been warned against, and falls through a weak part in the ceiling of what must be a monstrous cave. A darkness that's been there waiting for years. The fall is forty feet, onto a floor of jagged rock.

Upon impact, the bones of the boy's legs shatter into gravel, along with his pelvis, his right arm, most of the ribs on his left side. Because of the devastating violence of the skull fracture, however, the boy is spared the pain. The blood now coating his brain catches him softly in a continuation of his daydream instead, and time dilates for him, allowing him not just to live through adolescence and adulthood in a rush, but to graduate from that as a spirit of vengeance, a crusader in an elaborate costume, leveling the scales of justice but never resorting to guns. Over the barrel of a gun, this grown-up version of the boy would only ever see two people, he knows.

So he patrols the city every night with his unlikely boomerangs and grappling hooks and his endless menagerie of vehicles, waging an endless battle, fighting for the weak at great personal cost—the hematoma is pushing through his right cortex, now, and somewhere above the faithful butler is scrambling over rocks, calling a name desperately, insisting with his tone that the young master *be* there, please—and when the thugs and repeat offenders are no longer enough to sustain this last brave act of imagination, the boy calls on the radio shows he listened to once upon a time, and paints his foes gaudy and larger than life. He paints villains that are grand enough to be worthy of the injustice he felt outside the theater that night, and then he battles them tooth and nail night after night all across the city, diving from building to building, falling again and again only to get up one more time, one last time, and his story, his life, it lasts just as long as he can keep coming up with more capers to foil, just as long it takes for his eyes to register that the sharp-edged splotches flapping and screaming and swirling up to the light have a name, one he can almost hold onto.

THE TALK

It was late in the summer after the boy next door had hit a baseball through his own bedroom window. Ten o'clock maybe, the stars all out. A Friday. Dan was testing out his new (used) hot tub for the second night in a row. Because she didn't have school tomorrow, his daughter Shaney was testing it with him. They were in opposite corners, Shaney wearing the one-piece for his sake, he knew. He wasn't giving her any sips of his beer, though. Her hair was pinned up so it wouldn't turn green like her mother's: Dan was still trying to get the chemicals balanced. In five years it would be a joke. Right now though, his wife Sherry was parked in the living room, not talking to him. He had to concentrate to keep from smiling about it.

He leaned his head back, stared straight up, Shaney talking all the while, updating him on the complicated politics of—he was pretty sure—cheerleading try-outs. How this year the new coordinator was having all the girls try out again. Nobody was carrying over, like it had always been.

It was the first part of her case for new somethings, Dan knew: shoes, boots, piercings. It might even be leading up to the Sunfire for sale down the street, the one she'd been trying to bring up for days already.

Meanwhile, the water coursed around him, hot and perfect, and it didn't smell so much like chlorine now, and with this to come home to every night now, the days were going to be easier to get through, he knew.

"Dad?"

Dan cranked his head back to Shaney.

"I was just telling you about how James was saying you can't get pregnant that way."

Dan shook his head. It was her new trick, making him uncomfortable.

"You were talking about Ms. Glynnis," he said. "The new coordinator."

"She thinks she has to change everything."

Dan shrugged, tipped his beer up and held it there long enough that maybe Shaney would think he was agreeing, that he had some stake in the new and controversial policies of Ms. Glynnis.

"You know you'll make it," he said. "C'mon, I mean. Get serious."

"That's what I'm saying. Just because I was on last year—"

"You'll make it because you're you," Dan said, and then they were interrupted by a sound next door.

The boy with the broken window's light was on.

"Late," Dan said, staring.

"He's five, Dad," Shaney said.

Dan focused on the window, unsure how the kid being five was any kind of answer. For a moment he wondered how many beers he'd had, but then knew it couldn't be more than six, anyway.

And then it started.

The couple next door had crept into their son's room, to make use of his bunk bed. The lower level, it sounded like, probably so one of them could hang from the top rails. Something like that. The kid asleep on the couch, bathed in cartoon light.

Dan knew it was a bunk bed because they'd called him over to look at the window, like he knew anything about windows.

Shaney tried to swallow her laugh, but it came out her nose anyway.

The reason they could hear the couple so well was the baseball-sized hole in the glass. Duct tape kept the rain and the spiders out, but couldn't keep the wife's voice in.

What she was saying, too—Dan had to try not to smile.

And then it went on and on and on, the bed scraping and rattling, and all Dan could do, really, was stare at the surface of the water, and not let his feet touch Shaney's.

After six minutes of it, maybe, a crescendo of strained breathing seeping out a broken window, the lights came on. And then the bathroom light.

Dan shook his head, kept his eyes narrow. Pushed his lower lip out with his tongue.

When he looked up to Shaney, she collapsed into laughter.

Dan tipped his bottle up again, even though it'd been empty now for five minutes.

"Maybe I should fix that for them," he said.

"The window or the bed?" Shaney said, smiling far too wide.

And then she stood up from the water, and Dan looked away like he always did, and drank from his empty bottle again.

Wrapped in her towel, Shaney handed him another from the cooler.

He nodded thanks, tipped his head next door.

"I don't want to hear you on the phone about that," he said.

Shaney looked over for the briefest instant, pulled her top lip into her mouth, and told him in all seriousness *You won't,* then skipped inside, to whatever fifteen-year-old girls do at home at ten-thirty on a Friday night, and, after that, Dan knew better than to ever ask her any question he didn't already know the answer to.

NEITHER HEADS NOR TAILS

My father lost his left nipple in a hunting-related accident. He said it didn't make him any less of a father—it made him more of a man, really. What happened was it was still hot two weeks before bow season opened, and he was in the garage in his undershirt, limbering up his favorite bow. After a couple of half-draws to get the limbs warm he pulled the string back all the way, no arrow, and held it for a steady ten-count. On eleven, though, his shaky fingers let the bowstring slip. It sliced forward like razor wire. His nipple spun through the air, slapped the wall of the garage, and stuck. The way he tells it he kind of grunted a smile then—the nerves in his new cavity were still too shocked to relay anything up to his head—and walked directly inside, cupping his hand over his chest to keep the air out. By the time he got a towel and made it back to the garage, which he'd had open, Telly, our golden retriever, was sitting there, sweeping the concrete with his matted palm frond of a tail. My father could see that what Telly was trying to do was what he always did when he was guilty: gulping down his smile. There was still a wet smear on the wall where he'd licked the nipple off. It didn't make him any less of a dog, my father says. Really, it made him more of a dog, probably. And it's not like they could have sewn it back on anyway, right? And risked getting it back on but rotated half-around now, like a dial? No, and anyway, my father and his nipple stump—does it make me any less of a son for staring at it when we're at the beach? "Oh, that," my mom says when she sees the fascination in my face, and then tells my father to be sure and get the sunblock down into that, dear. That's the kind of place a cancer will just *pool*, if you let it. Because it's easier to play along, my father dollops the sunblock in, around, and after it's slick then, and we're all just lying there in the sun waiting to get dry enough for the drive home, I'll sometimes cue into my father's right hand, slapped across his chest like there's a flag in the area. But there's not. And he's asleep anyway, his right finger just skating around the oily rim of his caldera of scar tissue, that divot in his life.

What it does—and this is the part I mostly hate—is make me sneak touches up onto my own chest. Sneak touches and maybe even a light pinch, just to be sure, at least until my mom slaps the back of my hand and hisses *Not in public* to me.

It doesn't make me any less of a man, I don't think. But it doesn't help either.

THE LEPIDOPTERISTS

Assembly that day was the third and fourth graders all in the auditorium, probably thirty-five kids, total. It was supposed to have been about butterflies, but instead was a police officer and a counselor, because Morgan Falk's mom had shot his dad, put him in the hospital and probably a wheelchair, and now Morgan was living with his aunt, and nobody was to ask him about any of this when he came back to school tomorrow, got it? The police officer explained about "domestic abuse," and, out in the whispering and foot scraping of the forty students, Ian mouthed that bulky term to himself.

He never knew there was a name for his dad.

The police officer explained how Mrs. Falk was probably going to jail, because you can't just shoot people—you're supposed to call officers like him. Everybody understand?

Ian thought he did, yes.

That night he and his mom had to stay with *his* aunt when his mom heard that his dad had been in a fight at work that day. Her sister made them park in the garage, because she didn't want her front door kicked in again.

Ian's dad was waiting for him at the curb after school the next day. Ian's mom was sitting in the passenger seat of the truck. Her

23

hands were in her lap and her eyes were straight ahead, her lips a thin line.

Ian's dad stepped out so Ian could crawl in, sit between, and the rest of the afternoon was Ian's dad making up to them, being so nice it kept making Ian's mom gasp her breath in.

After Ian was in bed, he heard the phone crashing into its receiver on the wall over and over until something shattered. Instead of sleeping, he pinched himself awake until the house was quiet, and then he tiptoed out the screen door to his dad's truck.

Under the seat he found what he needed, its metal cold but warming almost instantly.

In his dad's shop, he considered all the tools on their hooks in the pegboard. He wasn't to ever touch these tools, they were his dad's living, but the utility knife wasn't even *on* a hook, was it? It was just laying there by the vice.

Ian slid it off, ran the blade in and out to be sure it was there. Back in the kitchen, he rubbed the top of his arm with a cube of ice until it was numb and then he made himself cut a fast X in the skin, deep enough that the muscle stretched back like it wanted to keep opening and keep opening.

The blood slid down his arm like a red sleeve unfurling, and before he could let himself think, he shoved his other hand into his pants pocket for the warm bullet he'd taken from his dad's truck.

He held it along the deeper part of the X he'd cut and pushed it in as best he could, his throat trying to throw up, tears streaming down his face, a moan coming from his mouth.

When the bullet wouldn't stay after he let it go, he opened the utility knife farther, all the way, and sawed deeper into his meat, his vision greying, his scream a ball in his throat he couldn't swallow. He was already sitting down or he would be falling over, he knew. Falling over and calling for his mom.

But he couldn't, he wouldn't. He had to do this.

Now the long arm of the X was deep enough.

He worked the little golden bullet in, clapped his hand over it, and called the number the officer at assembly had told him to call.

When the police car showed up, Ian's dad bellowed down the hall and rushed the door, his pistol by his leg.

Ian's mom ran to Ian in the kitchen. He was sitting in a pool of his own blood. It's where Ian's dad and the police officer from assembly found them. The police officer was the same one from assembly. He had Ian's dad's pistol, now.

"Son?" the police officer said.

"What?" Ian's dad said, stepping back, his hands held up, out of this, whatever it was.

"*Jim!*" Ian's mom screamed at Ian's dad, drops of saliva misting out in front of her mouth.

"Let me see," the police officer said, taking a knee.

When he pried Ian's hand away from his shoulder, the bullet squeezed out, tinked onto the kitchen floor.

"He shot me," Ian said about his dad. "He goes to jail now, right? That's what you said?"

Ian's mom hugged him to her, turning her back to the police officer and Ian's dad, her whole body shuddering with her sobs, and the police officer used the pencil behind his ear to lift the bullet up from the blood.

"You want me to believe he shot you with a *shell casing*, son?" the officer said, holding the pencil up, the golden bullet like a cap over the eraser, and Ian looked to his mom, not under-standing, and his mom just pulled them deeper into the corner they were already in.

"Nice try," his dad said with a chuckle, and so the officer left, and the part of the story of his scar Ian never tells is that the next year, in fourth grade, Morgan Falk, whose dad wasn't in a wheelchair but the cemetery, punched him right on that spot in the hall outside math one day, and that flash of pain was so exquisite, so perfect, that the two of them exploded into a cloud of butterflies and just hung there in the air, fluttering, weightless, becoming everything their mothers had wanted for them—two boys without a care—but then, as they had to, they drifted into class to fail another quiz, drifted into fights under bleachers, drifted into weekends in lockup, drifted into their *own* wives and kids, and though they would see each other nearly every week for the rest of their lives, going to and from this and that job, they would never speak of this moment, but each, on their deathbeds, would remember it, and try to smuggle it through with them, their hands cupped around it to keep it safe.

HANSOM IS

I was the first one to start painting eyes on the back of my horse's blinders. Soon enough Tedlow's gelding was wearing sunglasses, though, then Martinov's dun was sporting a stovepipe hat, and when Dominguez ordered that custom Spanish bit with the hole bored into it for a cigar (off-center, of course), I just held my hands up and turned around in my seat. On the back of my newly-shaved head, though, was a greasepaint smile, a pair of eyes, a nose that had been hard to get right in my series of five a.m. mirrors, but worth it, too. I tell my passengers that I'm a ventriloquist, talking without my lips, see, then stare lidlessly right at them for the rest of the ride, daring them to push me farther. By the end of the day, Martinov has two dummy arms spidering out of his side, holding the reins for him while he points to landmarks, and Tedlow's killed himself, his horse running wide-nostriled through the streets, and then the magnesium horse shoes Domingez ordered finally come special delivery, and her Wally's hooves spark with each step like he's walking on fire, like we all are, and I feel the back of my scalp contract in a smile, because we have the whole world before us, and then when a pair of hands cup over my eyes it just feels so right that I let the reins go slack and follow my horse into the night, both of us blind with wonder.

FABERGÉ

and then there was the day the week the year my mother found
the magazine I had hidden in such a perfect place, shuffled in
with the rest of my magazines, and I don't think she even told
me at first but thought about it for a week, maybe two, looked
at herself in the mirror a little too long some mornings, was too
polite to me about staring into the refrigerator for minutes on
end, and she never told my dad, either, but that was just because
he was dead already so maybe he knew anyway, in the way
dead people know things, which makes our skulls into glass so
he already knows my theory of masturbation, my theory that,
when a woman dies, no matter how old she is, how married,
how religious, instead of her life flashing before her eyes she
gets snapshots of every boy or man who's ever thought about her
alone, with lubrication, and how this means that some women,
they just die forever, and are maybe happy, or maybe they don't
care, and my dad, from the cockpit of the plane he's probably
still trying to pull out of that dive, he knows this about me I
know, that this is what I think, and not if he wrecks but *when* he
wrecks, like he's been doing since I was twelve and it happened,
three years ago, he'll know about this theory of masturbation
and smile behind the mic he should be screaming into, because

one corollary of my theory is that he's not really dying here, that, when his wife my mom finally dies, he'll live again, and not just for an instant, but for all those years he was just watching her across the cafeteria, and I'm there too with my tray, giving this to him, all I can, Dad, and it makes it easier for me when my mom finally confronts me about the pornography in her house, how she doesn't understand boys, won't even pretend to, and the magazine is there in her hands somehow, rolled to hide the cover, the same way I had to roll it after I bought it, because the store and the parking lot and the street were all so suddenly full of staring people, and then she does the thing I'm not expecting, she opens it not to the centerfold, the obvious material, but to the full-page girl back before the classifieds, standing there naked from head to foot, and I guess my mom knows this girl's my girl because of the way the stapled-spine is worn, or because the page is dog-eared, or I don't care how but she knows, and we look at each other and I can tell that she's proud of me the littlest possible bit, because this is maybe the only girl in the magazine whose inner thighs are touching, the only one looking at the camera instead of through it, and then—no words—she gives it back to me, says she doesn't want to find it again, and I can't even say anything like I usually do, anything like *don't worry, you won't, or then maybe don't come in my room?* and because I'm not saying any of that I just roll the magazine back up, sulk up to my room, and don't even open it for two days, the longest I've gone since I bought it, but then when I finally do it's with the window open, the lotion in the bathroom, and I could be reading anything, not looking at her, but, too, she's the only place left anymore, and it's not about the underswell of her breasts or the flare of her hips, the skin stretched tight across her pelvic bones, was never about any of that, but about the prop she's holding for some reason: a small, single-engine plane, its nose turned down into a dive I know I know, and through its cockpit window there's a man pulling back on the yoke, a magazine open on the seat beside him of another naked woman, holding another tiny plane, and on and on, furious, until I have to close my eyes to see the rest.

THE TWO-WOLF LIFE

My grandfather pulled me aside once to tell me that inside I had two wolves. Then he told me that, really, there shouldn't be *any* wolves. Number one, you're a male human, not a pregnant wolf. Number two, how did they even get in? Number three, how do they both fit? Number four, don't they need to breathe air? He ended this grandfatherly advice session by recommending I not tell anyone this two-wolf situation I was in, as they probably wouldn't believe me anyway, and that I should seriously consider seeing a doctor and a wildlife biologist, probably in that order. Most important, I wasn't to feed these wolves, as that would just mean they need to do their business after a few hours, since canine digestive systems are short. Then he told me that once he got drunk enough that he woke with a dead goldfish in his mouth, but that was just one animal, a dead one at that, and all he had to do was spit it out. So our two conditions didn't really match up. "Be careful, grandson," he said, holding me by both shoulders and staring into my eyes to be sure I was listening to him. Well, either that or he was trying to peer in, see a wolf looking back at him. I wanted to snap my teeth at him, just to give him a jolt, but I wasn't sure if it was me wanting to play that kind of joke, or one of those wolves inside me, so I just nodded Thanks, Granddad, and watched him walk away, not sure how he'd even known about my wolves in the first place.

THIRSTY

I have become used to the sight of my neighbor in a bra. That last sentence is a lie. What would not be a lie is that I stand in the kitchen "getting water" every weeknight between ten-thirty and eleven. I stand there the whole thirty minutes, as if the water is running. As far as she's concerned, my water *is* running, and I am getting some; from her window, my faucet is invisible. In these later years of my thirties, I have become a mime, yes, my hand continually reaching forward to the idea of a faucet handle, rather than the faucet itself. What would also not be a lie is that sometimes I'm caught at the sink, as it were, in my boxers. The term for this would be shared intimacy, I believe. Casualness about states of undress. Casual enough, indeed, that, after a few nights, I realize that if my neighbor can't see the faucet from her window while she drinks her water in her bra, then she also can't see my right hand—can't see the front of my boxers at all. Which presents certain opportunities. Considering that she might indeed be prolonging her bedtime drink of water due to what she might be considering *my* nudity, you could say that helps matters along, as it were. The only difficulty, of course, it's not disposal, as is usually the case in these situations—I am at the sink, and the water *does* turn on—it's timing, it's pacing, it's utilizing the memory of her bra last night to keep me at the edge as this night's bra surely approaches. It's being ready to accelerate or slow down the instant the light comes on in her kitchen. Except of course to get to the kitchen, she must first light up the hall, which is actually the proper point to, as it were, begin the more serious negotiations below her eye-level. The hard part? It's keeping my face the same. Pretending to be only thirsty, not in love well past the point of public decency, as her neighbor one flight up could surely attest to, were he not involved in his own nightly negotiations.

MY HOMETOWN

The security guard carries a white balloon on his nightly rounds. You can sit on the top of the gazebo just north of the town square and see him moving through the zoo. Nobody knows if it's the same balloon each night or a different one. White is the least common color, though. Down the spine of a beer bottle (where the paper label overlaps itself) the balloon looks like the pale crown of a tall bald man stopping at each of the cages to peer over the top at the animal within, perhaps retracing one, good, childhood outing. As far as we know, too, there's been no helium on the zoo grounds since the hyena incident, so we have to assume the security guard is a smoker, filling the balloon with his heated breath. Maybe it lasts just long enough for him to make his rounds, or maybe he stops at the crocodile pool, pulling on a cigarette under their lidless gaze then blowing into the sphincter of his balloon the way you blow into your fighting cock, which is with your eyes closed in prayer.

Our children aren't too young to be seduced by him, either, the security guard. On any given Halloween each street will have at least one police uniform adapted for zoo-use, balloon in tow. Some of the older kids—lanky and pale—even pretend to be the tall bald man the balloon almost is, but we discourage this, would rather they smoked cigarettes and took the beer we leave on the seats of our cars for them when we go hand over hand up the gazebo's rain gutter.

As far back as anyone can remember, too, no one's ever broken into the zoo—not us, or the class before us, who did it all, or the class before them—though one night of every year the walls of the zoo are supposed to expand out to the city limits signs, and then comes a man with a balloon, shining his flashlight into each of our windows, our faces, our dull eyes, before moving on, leaving us to our eating and mating and pacing. Some of our houses are fourteen hundred and fifty-six feet square, and some are eighteen hundred and twenty-two, and we know each of those feet so well.

THE PORNIEST PORN IN PORNTOWN

The woman's name was lost in The Fall, as was so much else we once thought vital—seasons, rivers, uncharred air—but her image persists, has become indelible. The giant wall of white upon which her travesties are projected once yearly has become a mecca for all in this, our new world. The desert for miles around is littered with the bleached bones of those who would gaze upon her bare body, to confirm for themselves and their outposts that one such as her ever actually existed. The recording of her on the giant wall of white doesn't exceed a count of 160, and it starts as it ends, with the sound of water slipping away by the *gallon*, if such a thing doesn't beggar the imagination, or hollow out the soul. Such heedless profligacy is of course the initial, albeit illicit draw to a recording as vile as this one surely is. But, sitting on the humps rising and falling before this giant wall of white, which we all know to be the grave mounds of the first congregants, who died upon viewing something so shocking as this—watch on, fellow pilgrims. It gets worse. Witnessing an act so obscene is penance, as this woman of course must be one of our ancestors, and thus tied to us by history and blood, if not culture and privation. If we would not repeat, then we must not look away. After disrobing and presenting her bare shoulders to us, so as to assure she has no open sores, no growths or parasites, she steps into what can only be called The Chamber. You can divine its religious significance by the regularity of the stones used to encase her on three sides, the fourth serving as a ritual flap to gain entry through. The animal from which such translucent skin might be harvested no longer walks our world. Though foggy and indistinct for a moment, this woman—pale of skin, short of hair, light of manner—kneels to an instrument too sacred to be seen directly, but which produces the next stage of this impossible act. This is the part in the recording where all arranged on the grave mounds either gasp or become, for the rest of the recording, incapable of breath, as what's now on screen is as sacrilegious as it is compelling: *water* streams forth in a regular stream of unceasing droplets from the inverted silver chalice extending from the forewall of The Chamber. The woman closes her eyes so as to protect them, and, to a person, each pilgrim washing themselves in the entrancing glow of this heresy finds themselves incapable of not rubbing their own forearms and shoulders, imagining chambers such as this still exist, and water is obtainable for more than a spoon at a time, is so available, in fact, that it can be used like *this*. And the woman herself, as if aware of us out here, soaking this in, her pleasure in this unstopping stream of water, it's not only apparent, it's infectious. But when she turns her open mouth to this unending torrent? This is when the crowd arrayed before her raises their voices in anger, demanding she *Drink, drink!* How could anyone resist, from a source such as this? Of course, however, this woman doesn't. This is why children are brought to learn from this recording. When the water continues to spill, shining on her skin but slipping away, uncaught, never to be used again . . . this is when the Rationer appears. Her tall shape is smoky through the opaque flap, her face indistinct, her hair pulled back in a bun of sorts, her dress drab and unwashed, but her knife, falling into this degenerate woman's unmarred flesh, it's sharp. It's sharp enough. Of the people gathered to watch this denuded, wasteful woman punished thusly by the Rationer, there's always one who stands when the stabbing starts, stands not just to cheer, but to roar with the righteousness of this act. And then all are rising to support the Rationer's judgment, lest they themselves find her smoky form halfway behind them when they let a drop of their day's second gulp of water wet their dusty chin instead of their parched throat. As the woman's life is being cut away in pieces, so does the recording itself shatter into smaller and faster pieces with each stroke of the Rationer's blade, until, as must happen, the woman falls dead over the side of her chamber, grasping onto the flap in what must be regret, the wish to have done better with such a gift. Here, lest we forget the intent and import of this recording, we look into the hole at the bottom of her erstwhile chamber, which is when the crowd, as a single person, falls to their knees in sympathetic pain at this unending waste they can't stop: the water, still streaming from its high-mounted silver chalice, is now spiraling down into that open throat at the bottom of The Chamber, surely to fall into the void, and never get imbibed by man nor beast nor plant—the greatest sin of all. The great white wall this plays on is of course chipped and showing divots, as, when the recording settles back on the woman's dead eye, itself forced to witness this travesty, whatever item is at hand is flung up into the finger of light delivering her. Others, however, rapt in this recording, aroused by the nurturing wetness on display and not heeding the consequences, driven to frenzy by this glimpse of What Once Was, they couple in the light falling down onto them, and the children conceived in such manner will themselves one day be led by the hand to these rolling grave mounds, to gaze in rapt wonder up at this, their little hands curling into fists, wishing it was them stabbing her, but any tears of rage they let slip, they of course know to save them, for the good of all.

HATCHERY

Martin had once tried to shoot a fish he put in a barrel. The first two shots, through the rusted bottom of the barrel—55 gallon drum, really, one of his father's—would have drained it after a few hours, but Martin wasn't that patient: tracking the silver flash of the fish with his shotgun, following the fish up the side of the barrel, to the water's surface, he shot his best friend Grandy in the shin, turning his whole lower leg to tatters. As punishment, Martin's father made him wash Grandy's blood from the air-drowned, otherwise unharmed fish, cook it, then eat it for dinner. Martin was done long minutes before his father set his own fork down, said to him, "So you learn your lesson then?"

Martin looked down to his empty plate, studied it for the right answer, then nodded, said to his father yes, yes sir. He should have used a bigger fish, sir.

His father tried to hide his smile, failed, then clapped his son on the shoulder, used that hand to box him on the ear, and pulled Martin close to tell him not to be a smart ass, son. *Obviously* there should have been less water in the barrel, right? Or a smaller barrel?

Martin, his eye watering in sympathy with his boxed ear, shrugged, tasted the fish on the back of his throat, and didn't tell his father the truth. It wasn't that he knew the saying was about enough fish in one place that you couldn't *help* hitting one, but that when he raised the barrel of his shotgun along that one fish's path, he knew it was tracing the lines of Grandy's lower leg.

The real saying, he knew, should really be along the lines of how, if you filled a dead bird with lead pellets then hurled it from a moving car into the plate glass window of a barbershop, everybody would think the bird had just flown there itself.

Martin rubbed his hot ear and walked down to the creek for another fish.

THE SADNESS OF TWO PEOPLE MEETING IN A BAR

For a moment the crowd parts and they see each other, him at the bar, her on the wall, but it's not long enough to tell if they're attached. She gets a cigarette going, he orders another beer, the pads of his fingers leaving smears on his frosted mug, and they watch each other, and let each other look—him standing once, pretending to try to see the game on the television better, her in turn angling herself sideways, as if she's just seen a friend through the plate glass. Twenty minutes later they've sidled into their places beside each other, and the bartender knows what to do, and her friend knows what not to do, and the only two people in the whole place suddenly unable to open their mouths, form the right words right then, are him and her, because they're seeing it like a movie already: that she has a husband she doesn't want anymore but can't throw away. That he's only in town for two weeks, recovering from something he can't really talk about. Something dark and suggestive. That, over the course of the next two nights, after she surrenders her body to him in the parking lot, he'll become addicted to her enough to ask her to run away with him. But she can't: her husband. So, a plan, a diagram, the husband alive at point A, dead in a trunk by C. Then the house and the land and the fortune is theirs, but soon enough *his* plan eases into motion: to come to the city, find a rich, needy girl, get her to marry him, and then, six months later, stage her suicide, inherit her money. But the husband, maybe he never really dies in the trunk of the car that goes into the pond. Maybe he was just in the kind of debt he could only hide from in an obituary. And maybe the dark and suggestive thing in the new husband's past was a formerly rich, now-disfigured woman, who finds the not-really-dead husband staking out the new honeymooners, and they're in a bar, of course, oblivious, and the two wronged *not*-dead people swear vengeance together, the bartender as witness, but their plan has so many machinations, finally, that, in the boat-explosion (Step G), everyone wakes swimming in the moonlight, nameless with amnesia, and suddenly they don't know who to save anymore, who has priority—the woman with the patch over her eye? the man with the gun?—and so wander off into the city to their separate dooms, their individual rags-to-riches stories, the baby one of them doesn't know about, the dog waiting to reunite with its owner.

In a moment as long as a dart arcing towards the board, the two of them see this, but she doesn't draw the back of her hand away from his third knuckle, where he's accidentally brushing her, and he doesn't stop reaching for his drink.

"I can leave," he offers, not looking quite at her, and in answer she takes his cigarette, the dart nosing into a bent green rectangle on the board behind them, and whispers that she doesn't have a dog, *does he?* and because of this they think they can beat it this time, stay one step ahead, so they race hand in hand into the parking lot, leaving the bartender behind them cleaning his glass, the dishrag wrapped tight around the hook his hand is now, the dart board bristling with darts thrown by the woman with the leather patch over her eye, and nothing ever really stops, you just have to decide where to get off.

HOW TO KNOW YOU'RE A KILLER

1.) You're a killer because you say "Goodbye, *Tiffany*," to the college girl passing your butter and white bread across the scanner at the grocery store, even though her name tag is scarred and beaten and only visible in flashes under the windbreaker she's got on because the register is right by the front door, and the front door is always hissing open, sometimes even when nobody's there.

2.) You're a killer because you let the mouse go that shows up on your glue trap under the sink, and you stand there and watch it to see what it's going to do now, in the alley, where it's going to go, and how, since its four feet are now four tufts of grey on the glue trap you've stuck to the side of the scarred and beaten dumpster. Mouse bones are like wet toothpicks. Just scissors.

3.) You're a killer because you think about your brother at odd moments, about the way his name tasted in the air when your mother would call it, like it stood for both of you, like you would of course follow wherever he went, like you liked eating mashed potatoes and casserole as much as he did, but you didn't, you couldn't. In those scarred and beaten dishes you only ever saw all the hundred other casseroles that had lived there, and died there.

4.)   You're a killer because you know to never look away when an off-duty police officer locks eyes with you at a stop sign, his instincts ringing all his bells, and nobody even had to tell you not to look away, you just know this from your *own* instincts, you know that his scarred and beaten soul, that it's calling across to yours, that it's the same kind of lonely and afraid. Just pull forward when it's your turn. Keep moving.

5.)   You know you're a killer because you never can remember the plots of the movies you sit through at the second-farthest theater from your apartment, but you can list the color and pattern of every shirt the two leads wore, because that's where the real story was, it was in those selections, it was like standing before a closet for you, standing there and parting the shirts, looking behind them, to the wardrobe designer, the one you waited until the end of the credits to find. A name you say later in your bedroom, in secret, like a promise.

6.)   You're a killer because you know the truth about Batman, about why he works at night, and why the mask, the gear, all the complicated exit strategies, and why he never uses guns—they attract too much attention—and, most of all, why he's always watching, and why his mouth when he's watching is so important. And why he needs a cave like that. And why this scarred and battered city, it's his and his alone.

7.)   Another way you know you're killer through and through is that you can't stop with the lists, they're everywhere, and they're all so necessary, they're all so perfect, so elegant, so right, they each take so many drafts to *get* them that right, but the main way you know you're a killer is that you're not on a single one of these lists.

8.)   The eighth way you know you are what you are is that when your brother dared you to eat that Christmas light bulb in fifth grade you did, not little by little like he meant, but all at once, like a glass chili pepper from the cafeteria, and then he had to pay you like he said, only, that night, you crept across to his bed, your mouth still bloody, and you slid that scarred and battered five dollar bill under his pillow, and never asked him if he found it.

9.)   You know you're a killer because of the way you can feel the whole city watching you push your shopping cart past the scarred and battered meat cooler at the grocery store, your eyes and mind and privates not not *not* catching on the slash of white rib bone coming up through the red meat, you're not looking at all, you're just walking past, your legs working just like everybody else's, just like normal.

10.) You know all this, can feel your true self writhing around in your chest, but a list doesn't prove anything, does it? No, what proves it finally is that you've sat in the back seat of a scarred and battered car for three hours now, a name on your lips to say when her shift's over, and she's behind the wheel: "Melissa." Not "Tiffany." It's so she'll think this is all a mistake. So she'll think this doesn't have to be happening. But it does. It already is. The look in her eyes in the rearview, it's going to be perfect.

THE WAGES: AN ARGUMENT

thesis

At twelve years old he was at the lake. Colorado. Playing hide and seek or war or something with his brother, lots of running through the bushes, getting farther and farther away from the truck. His brother who was three years younger than him. The shape of the part of the lake they were at was like a finger reaching into land, and all the green things grew right up to the water. He was twelve years old; he wasn't thinking anything, he was thinking maybe about his little brother, the way their hair was the same, dark and shiny and fine. It would make a ring in the sun that stayed level even when his head moved, his eyes always looking somewhere else.

They were running in the trees now.

He was ahead of his brother but not by much, but enough that for a moment, when he stumbled out into tall grass and sunlight he was alone, blinking, and he could hear them coming, right out of the pages of *National Geographic,* manifesting first as heads balanced on long necks and then as things driven by men on horseback—llamas—and for as long as he stood there with them streaming by he could believe anything.

antithesis

At fourteen years old he was sitting at the breakfast table waiting for his pants to warm in the dryer. It was exactly eight days after his dad walked out of a bar and shot himself in the cab of his truck. At school no one talked to him. He could do whatever he wanted; he stared into his locker. His pants were tumbling four feet away, the only thing in this morning. His mother walked past them, past the dryer, to the porch with her first cup of coffee, then returned, waited for him to finish his cereal in a way that he knew that's just what she was doing. When he was done she told him their kitten had had a kitten of her own, evidently. Just one. It was on the porch. She told him twice that she couldn't do it. He nodded okay.

On the porch the kitten was still breathing. No hair no eyes.

His mom offered him the gun through the screen door but he couldn't, because it would spook the horses, and he had to get to school. So he picked the kitten up with the flat-bottomed shovel and carried it to the burn barrels, where there was a small concrete pad. It was cold. His breath hung white in front of his face. Because he was wearing basketball shorts and boots without socks the kitten when he slammed the cinder block down was wet on his legs, and warm, and he didn't tell any of them about it.

synthesis

At twenty-six years old he was sleeping in a queen bed with his wife. He slept with his toe on her heel, the same trick he'd used with his brothers when he was young, to make sure they were there. His brothers were all in different states now; he had stayed within a hundred miles of home. He woke silently a little after two, and he lay there breathing until almost four.

Telling himself to breathe. When his wife asked him was he

okay he told her yes the first two times, but then on the third he didn't answer, and she sat up and he didn't ask her if he'd ever killed anyone one drunk night with a trashcan lid, but he did tell her that he had that memory, all smeared around in his head. Of placing that person with a face in plastic under the kitchen floor of a rent house.

His wife told him that she was with him all the time back then, that that never could have happened, that, drinking, he wouldn't have planned ahead enough to take care of everything, that there would have been a smell, *something*, but then too she said that the only reason this seemed so real to him was that this is what he *does*, as a writer—that it was his job to anticipate all the details, all the excuses, anything that might expose the lie—and her voice coming at him across the darkness of the bed was the same as the llamas rushing past, only now they were going the other way.

WHERE WE LIVE

It got to where there were so many gravemounds that the dips between were standing water, and the kids would play in them, they would wage battles where they held each other under by the back of the head, and with their faces down there like that, their air gone, every day or two one of them would sputter up saying how they'd opened their eyes down there, they'd opened their eyes and they hadn't been alone, there had been fingers that maybe weren't longer than normal, not really, but were definitely more starved down, more dried out, more reaching, and we should have listened closer to these encounters, we should have believed, we should have known our kids were coming back with whole fingernails as secret treasure, and keeping them in boxes and cans and babyfood jars, jars they should have screwed the lids on tighter, because moths were drawn to them, moths and spiders, such that by week's end these jars were empty, these dead fingernails cocooned high in the corners we couldn't reach, corners we didn't know we *needed* to reach, but it might not have really mattered, either, it might have just fooled us into thinking we could have caught the beetles that hatched, that climbed into our mouths and noses and ears while we slept, crawled in and multiplied in the hundred hollow places of the human body so that a single cough would birth a storm of the biting gnats that seemed to always find their way to the crosses and markers and headstones of the gravemounds, to coat them as if forming a protective shell, as if whispering among themselves, or perhaps ignoring us en masse—the insect mind is impossible to know, if indeed they were insect—but their writhing intentions, they finally didn't matter as much as the fact that, when the dead under the water still standing between the gravemounds opened their mouths, they, the dead, were careful that each of their mouths admitted no water, could serve as a dry little chasm, a pit in the surface of the murk the insects could swarm down into, coating our deads' insides, migrating by artery and vein and capillary all the way to the ends of their decayed fingers, to the naked fingernail beds waiting there, beds the gnats could push themselves up through, thus providing shiny black nails for the hands stabbing up through the water in a series of tremendous splashes, for us, hands rising up to tell us it was time to move again, time to start over, time to walk away into the night, and then start to shuffle, and then to run into the blackness.

SEAFOOD

After examining the facts for eight-odd years, in which both his wife and his job fell away like a second, unnecessary skin he'd never even known he had, Rick finally decided that it had been obvious, really, and, being not just rational but bound by the smallest of indicators, he had no choice but to admit that that day he'd taken his four-year old son to the beach it had, yes, been almost solely to have him dragged out by a shark. If there had been a painting of that day, he knew, then he and Danny would have been at the center of it, every brushstroke radiating out from them. But there had been no painting, and he hadn't even known then to be looking for the brushstrokes—the way the car only started on the third try, the way the red light at the second intersection had buzzed. The hundreds of reflections of themselves smearing by in all the windows they passed. How Danny had asked if his friend down the street could come, and Rick had said no. It was like, at some level, a Rick inside of Rick— the one who had to keep living, maybe—had been able to read all this, but had gone ahead to the beach anyway. Had made the *decision* to go ahead to the beach. Because of stubbornness, Rick thought. Because it felt cavalier to buck fate, and win. To risk Danny's life. What he'd had for breakfast that morning was two slices of bread around some leftover meatloaf, still cold in the middle. That alone, he was pretty sure, should have been enough to keep him away from the water that day. It was like the world was warning him. Wouldn't the snooze on his alarm have worked better if he'd really been meant to take Danny to the beach? But it went back farther too, to the day before, the way his creamer had hung in his afternoon coffee instead of mixing in, and the week before, a cloud he remembered seeing on the way home from work, and, before that, January, when he'd been flipping through the channels and seen the ocean for about five seconds. And it even went back to when Danny was born— maybe Rick had been planning the shark then, in his fatherly way. He didn't doubt it. He was capable of anything, he knew, even eight more years of studying what he'd started calling The Prelude, teasing apart the facts layer after layer to get to the real truth of what had happened. Maybe even somewhere in there he would find the time to visit the empty grave, and say goodbye. But not today. When he was done, he told himself. When he'd figured it all out, when he understood why, and could explain it to Danny, and apologize for not having paid proper attention to the way the rearview mirror that morning had been angled down at the passenger seat. In the reflection, just for a moment, Danny had been looking away, out his window. Rick, though, killer that he was, just creaked it back to see behind him instead, like that was more important.

COPS & ROBBERS

My wife's glasses were driving her crazy, so before too long she started killing people in quiet ways. She was remarkably efficient. As a homicide detective, I had nothing but respect for her manners. However, the fact remained that she was breaking laws I was sworn to uphold. Over the next few years, then, we did the dance we were supposed to do—hunter, prey; prey, hunter; she almost but never quite falling for our many baits, me slamming my badge down on my captain's desk so many times that it bent the clasp—but at the end of the song we had to acknowledge that we were evenly matched. Any good marriage counselor would have told us the same thing. Our dinner talk and our pillow talk were formal, polite, model. We both washed our hands after work, commented in our individual ways on the bodies piling up in the newspaper, and kissed each other off into the city the next morning. Soon enough, retirement was looming before me, and she was the only active case I hadn't been able to close. At my farewell banquet she held my large hand in her smaller one, and then, that night in the foyer, the bulb overhead not yet warm, her mask slipped a bit, her killer's fingers reaching under my suit jacket, to my shoulder holster, but after twenty-five years on the force I was expecting this too. She came up from the formed leather not with my service revolver, but a pair of gold-rimmed reading glasses. They matched my new watch. She inspected them from every angle then lowered her face to them, looked up to me with them on—looked *out* of them to me—and said *nice*, turning to face object after object in the foyer, as if they were all new, and in this way we walked together into what was supposed to be our twilight years, but felt more like dawn.

MATINÉE: A LOVE AFFAIR

In the absence of traditional cinema we floundered from theatre to theatre, bleary-eyed, numb around the heart. It was the winter we wondered where all the crows went. The city was so white without them. We hid from it in lobbies and bathrooms and under marquees, rummaged in each others' clothes for warmth and didn't talk for two hours at a time, then let it out all at once, our breath visible before our faces.

All the ushers knew us by shape—the trench coat and the toboggan and the girl with the scarf trailing into the horizon—and we knew them too, had been them before, had even cultivated a stalk of corn when it grew up from the grate behind concessions, its hands imploring the false light. But it's not false, either. In the darkness of the theatre we did it too, stretching our fingertips up just to be a part of it, a brief shadow. Even walking home we would see ourselves silhouetted against a building by approaching headlights and smile, then cast our eyes down over it, trying to affect a forlorn posture before the car swept past.

Nothing romantic was lost on us. It was like we were in remission from something terminal or like we were recovering from something narcotic, or like we didn't have anywhere else to go. It wasn't bad to cry at the end, either, through the credits.

Not because the movie had done what it's supposed to do, what it always does, what it can't help doing, but because it was over.

In the coffee shops we would repeat them word for word, though, sitting across from each other, the toboggan smoking, the trench coat folded on the back of the booth, the scarf rolled into a muffler, a filter for the smoke she would never complain about, and then we would slouch off at dawn to our stations behind the counters of video stores, on the second floor of bookstores, on the phone selling impossible items to people who needed impossible items.

It goes without saying that we loved each other in such a way that in our individual beds we imagined the other two there, only they had their winter clothes on under the sheets. In the perfect theatre there's total darkness, just a finger of light pulsing into life on the screen, and the images that collect there are more real than a city snowblind without the necessary contrast of crows, so that you never want to lean up out of your seat, listen across the coffee shop to people who bunched over with you, saying things like *it was all they hoped for and less.*

The corn we grew that time we ate raw, with imitation butter and pretzel salt. It was a furtive act; we were gathered in the projection booth, celluloid passing by all around us at twenty-four feet per second, just fast enough for the still image to blur into motion, into magic. The theatre below us was empty but full of sound. We swore then never to leave it, to become part of the carpeted walls, the sloping floor, the ceiling forever unseen. After we had to leave for other jobs we still came back to walk the rows and the aisles, the empty cups and smuggled bottles snapping into our hands of their own accord, the whole place hushed save our breathing, our wonder.

In the natural light of day we blinked through the park. It goes without saying that the crows returned with the melting snow.

We didn't shed our clothes, though; they covered our gaunt ribs, hollow stomachs, the physical evidence of our emotional need. One day finally when the manager was pretending to sweep around us we opened our mouths for him like birds, heads tilted back over the movie seats, and in return he asked for our ticket stubs. We smiled—one of us closing their eyes in pleasure, defeat, *aptness*—then emptied our pockets in great heaping handfuls that fluttered down through our fingertips for him, and then we waded out, our sodas held high above our heads. Whatever spilled we didn't go back for.

In some places the crows live generation after generation behind the theatre, feeding off uncooked kernels until they can eat nothing else. That's where we were going.

THE BROACHING

"So what if you were like in a coma for two or three years, right?"

"Would you shave my legs for me?"

"I mean it would suck and all, but who would I have sex with?"

"You'd seriously be thinking that?"

"Not because I wanted to."

"You're asking for permission or something, aren't you? Is this about Marcy from work?"

"No, no, I just—I wouldn't want to feel like I was cheating on you. I'd want you to know it was purely, you know. Like, physical."

"So if you were in a coma, you're saying I could shack up with whoever, too? With *Danny*?"

"Not saying move in, you're getting all—I just mean like one night, yeah? Out of three years. Or five, you never know."

"And would I ever tell you? Would you ever tell me?"

"Hunh."

"Yeah."

"I guess we could. If we talk about it now, beforehand."

"I'm not planning any motorcycle wrecks any time soon."

"And Danny's not my vote."

"For me."

"For you, yeah."

"But it wouldn't just be one guy, right? Or, for you, one girl? I mean, you've got 'urges' and 'needs'—"

"We're both human."

"So what you're saying is, so long as it's not a repeat-thing, a standing Saturday and Wednesday rendezvous with the same person—"

"You'd get attached, then. I mean, I would too. Anybody would."

"Okay, I'm with you. Different people, purely sex, no feelings, like washing the windows or cutting the grass, just something that has to be done every so often . . ."

"I'd still come see you all the time, of course. We'd still have us."

"*You'd* have us. I might never wake up."

"Well?"

"Well what?"

"Are you in?"

"To your hypothetical no-guilt extra-marital flings of no consequence?"

"Just while the other one's in a coma or something."

"Or something. But what if I have surgery, and am recovering for like a week, and you see some commercial in the waiting room, get all hot and bothered?"

"We can write a document up, then, to cover all that. Sign it."

"Because married people are never bitter about contracts."

"I'm just saying."

"You're scared."

"Of losing you."

"Of losing what I've got. What every girl's got."

"Not every."

"Depends if it's been three weeks or three months, right?"

"I can write it up."

"So what if I just get the flu real bad, am down for like two and a half weeks, and my breath's all icky. Is that too long for you to wait for your beloved?"

"You're not being serious. Forget I said anything. I'm just trying to . . . if you're just going to do this, we can—"

"What if I wreck my van into a bridge and get whiplash—oh no, whiplash, she can't do anything for six weeks! Hurry, hurry, go to the slut store! Bring a coupon, here, take mine, use the drive-through window!"

"It wouldn't be like that."

"I don't even have a van."

"Such a safe document to sign, then, right?"

"There are bridges everywhere, though."

"I'll write it up, okay? And, you know."

"'Know?' Know what?"

"Oh, I mean, I'll like, post-date it—I mean *pre*, pre-date it. Whatever. For our anniversary, so it matches and we can remember it."

"Excuse me?"

"Just to make it as old as us."

"You're saying that would make it retroactive, aren't you? That it would grandfather the past in, as well as this little dream-coma vacation you're betting on?"

"I don't *want* it to happen."

"This *is* about Marcy, and her boots."

"Listen—"

"Oh, oh, oh! No. Oh *shit*. This is—what do you consider a 'coma,' right? That's what we're really talking about, isn't it? How were you going to word it?"

"What do you mean?"

"A coma means I'm where you can't reach me, can't have your precious sex with me, isn't that it?"

"I was just saying—"

"No, you were just saying that, for you, a coma is when I'm not around. Like, oh, I don't know, last *month*, when I had to go to Portland for two weeks? Tell me I'm wrong. Tell me Marcy was never over here. That I can call her right now and say something about how the silver on our fridge isn't as silver as it used to be, see if she has to think, to process from white to silver in her pretty little head."

"This isn't about her."

"Then who?"

"Us, just us."

"One of whom was effectively in what the other would conveniently consider a coma, the other of whom wants to stick his—"

"Worst case scenario, that's all I'm saying."

"Best case scenario?"

"What?"

"Want to know what your best case scenario is, darling dear? That when I invite Marcy over tonight after dinner to tell her about my fabulous trip, and ask her to run some cold water over a dish towel to dab at the wine I just spilled on the couch, that she doesn't know that our faucet's backwards."

"Please."

"No, no, this'll—I'll tell her it's too bad about your *herpes*, but that we're managing it. When a couple's committed, it can work. Yes, oh. I can't wait."

"Forget I said anything."

"No, don't—I want to sign this wonderful, magical document. If I was in a coma to you last month, then you were in a coma to me as well, weren't you? Did you think I was just going to stay in my hotel in Portland for that whole forever two weeks? Or, I mean, 'room.' I never actually left the hotel, I guess, unless you count that time in the parking garage. Did you know they just leave their shuttle unlocked all night? But those rails that hold the luggage in, they make excellent handles."

"Come on."

"This could really work out. We're forging new ground, new relationship territory. Oh, oh, I feel a sneeze coming on, you, you, you'd better get on the phone, the escort service can send somebody right over—"

"You're joking about Portland, aren't you?"

"Me? Oh, of course I am, dear. It's not like you can call every guest over to use our sink anyway, right?"

"I love you, you know."

"This is what love is. Love is what we're doing right now, isn't it? Just don't get hit by any trains on the way to the bathroom, there. Don't close the door either. I might not think you're coming back. Wouldn't want any misunderstandings now, would we? I can only abstain for so long. Maybe *I* should call Marcy for myself. For both of us at once, even."

"You're joking, right?"

"You're hoping I'm not, aren't you?"

"I'm going to use the bathroom."

"Careful, now. Maybe cough before you come back in? Or, does it even count if you're just on the phone, like . . . you know. Following orders?"

"Goodnight."

"Goodbye."

The lights go down.

THE DECOMPOSITION OF A CONVERSATION

My father would jump into the pool with a new cigarette dangling from his lips. He had an ashtray on the diving board. Like he wanted to be responsible with his smoking until the last possible moment, until he couldn't be responsible anymore. After his dive he would stay under for minutes it seemed, the grey-scum water smoothing out over him, the backyard absorbing his splash, and then he would crash through the surface, cling to the side. Cough another cigarette into action.

This isn't a cancer story. It's about religion.

The one truth my father gave me to order my life by was that we lack the proper enzymes to digest ourselves. Saying good-bye at the airport once he gave me a complicated gift, and I held it in my hand and called out to him as he was walking away, asking him if it would last.

"It's a Polaroid," he called back, as if I was looking too deep, "your mother," and fourteen years and two wives later his plane is still roaring off.

In the picture she's wearing mirrored sunglasses. And she wasn't going to die that next day or month or year and she's still alive now, a grandmother. The picture was taken at a parade, in the sun. I don't blame her for being there. My father did die of cancer, too, but that doesn't prove anything. My mother smuggled cigarettes into his room for him, even. My girlfriend says that's romantic, but the world's a romantic place to her.

I sit on the edge of the bed and try to tell her how it really was: the morning of the Polaroid I was the first to wake, to look over the tops of everybody sleeping in the sun-room. The Fourth of July, it was always The Fourth of July, all summer long. My father was the next to wake and half-asleep he told me about his own father, their big fishing trip, his main childhood memory: the two of them out on the lake, his father fumbling a beer into the water, diving in after it, pulling his old trick of pretending to drown, my father at twelve years old knowing it was a joke but all the same picturing his dead father under the boat with the bass jigs, floating beside them, his eyes glassy black like theirs, all their heads turned to the fireworks blossoming in the sky miles away.

My mother shushed him when she woke, and so my girlfriend will understand what I'm trying to tell her when I bend my arm like my mother did that morning, to show where the spider had laid its egg: in the crook of her elbow. We watched it all morning, following the red streaks up her arm. It was blood poisoning. The story was that when the red fingers reached your heart, they would make a fist, and that was it. Even the nurse on the phone said so.

But my mother.

She watched the fingers reaching for her, and in a casual voice asked how long the parade usually went?

My father smiled. "Two o'clock," he said, drawing hash lines on her arm with a felt tip pen he had to wet with his tongue.

It was still nine in the morning.

At the parade I was the one who took the Polaroid of her. In it she's looking up, establishing the pattern of my life, her eyes hidden, her purse arm swelling in the sun, too stiff to bend. A spider growing in there.

My girlfriend doesn't know what to say when I'm done so she covers herself like girls do in the movies when they realize they've made a mistake, and I turn away politely, say that my father was right, we don't have the proper enzymes to digest ourselves. But our parents can give them to us when no one's paying attention. Stepping into the shower to think or to not think—to be in a different environment than the bedroom—I cup my hand around a cigarette, know it won't last, but just for the rush of life I hold the smoke in as long as I can against the water, close my eyes.

TIME

She's changing shirts in the passenger seat of Gray's Firebird when the guy in the truck in the other lane sees. He leans forward, accelerates. It's just a black bra, she knows—a bikini top at the beach—but still, the shirt she's putting on now takes longer than it has to, and her back never touches the seat. Then she brushes the static from her hair. Gray looks over to her, then up to the road, then in the mirrors for cops, then raises his beer to his lips. The guy in the truck is gone, pushed back in traffic.

"This one," she says, about the exit—they're going to the house of a guy she knows who's supposed to have something— and Gray takes it.

"Sure?" he says, his hand to shifter.

"Up here," she says back.

It's a lie, their fourth exit in thirty minutes, but they've got all afternoon. If they get messed up too early, they'll be crashed by midnight, probably miss something good. A race, an arrest, somebody they haven't seen since high school. There are only so many exit ramps to take though, before Gray stops being the kind of polite he's being now. And he's not interested in anything else. She tried that too.

Ten minutes later, they're back on the interstate, Gray flattening the top of each gear out.

She lets two exits pass—wasting them, but she has to act like she knows—then directs him down another.

Gray downshifts, the nose of the car diving, engine climbing, then shows off in his quiet way, taking the sharp exit while checking the mirror to see if he can raise his can.

He doesn't take a drink, though.

"Huh," he says, still looking in the mirror.

She turns, to see what.

Behind them is the truck from before the last exit. The guy.

"He's following us?" she says.

"Wrecker," Gray shrugs. "Lost as we are, probably."

"I'm not lost, Gray."

"Yeah, well."

She turns back around in the seat.

"He's not either," she says.

Gray checks the mirror again.

"He saw me changing," she says. "My bra."

Gray looks at her, looks at her, then shakes his head no.

"Here, then," she says, taking them down a narrow road. The truck follows, its tow rig silhouetted against the concrete underpass for a moment.

Gray slams his open hand into the steering wheel, thins his lips.

She knows him too well to have to say anything. Five minutes later—two roads later, just to be sure, give the guy a chance—Gray scratches to a stop, the Firebird angled across the road, then rises from the car, already talking to the guy in the tow truck, not caring about the tools he has to have under the seat, the gun he might have in the glove compartment, how long this is going to take, and if she smiles when she pulls herself up out of the passenger seat, to watch, nobody knows.

DOORS & PASSAGEWAYS

There's a moment near the front of the house, between the closet and the front door, where there's just enough room to hold the closet door open, to keep it from closing on your mother, to keep your father from closing it on your mother again and again, but the floor's slick and the air full of voices and even together you and your mother can't outweigh him, outpush him, keep the door open.

There's a moment between your eleventh and twelfth years, between you and your mother and your father, between you and the front door and the hospital, and it would be easy to say it lasts for the rest of your life, is big enough to last the rest of your life, but if it lasts it's only because it becomes one moment with all the rest, indistinct. And you don't want it anyway. Better just to keep the door shut.

'TIS THE SEASON

My father, coming home all through December with dollar boxes of Christmas lights, the kind from the display at the liquor store, lights he would string on our tree while we slept, and beyond, draping across the couch, the curtain rod, the coat rack, finally tracing his steps after he's lost his bottle again, finds instead a place on the floor to sleep, the end of the green line of bulbs held ahead of him like he's still reaching, or doesn't want to forget where he was, or wants us to know that this is what he was doing, for us. All for us.

Such a festive guy. Such a good father.

The night we finally plugged all his lights in, the house went black with fuse death, and my mother sighed, unsurprised, and I felt my eyes cupping to accept this too, but then my father's hand tightened around mine, and I saw what he was seeing: on the mantle, half under the couch, balanced in the tree, perfect little squares of green. The price tags glued to the necks of all his lost bottles were glowing with the season.

It's not a reason to drink, I don't think.

But it's not a reason not to, either.

AUTOBIOGRAPHY

for Edward Isham

The way it works down here is simple: my father's seventeen, no job no nothing, coasting into a tarpaper convenience store on fumes when there's this tall bald guy holding a baby up, palmed in one hand. The baby's wearing a diaper that soaks up the sun; the man's arm is inky blue with tattoos. The woman trying to climb him has to be the kid's mother. It's the casual way the man smokes his cigarette that gets to my dad. Words are passed but they don't matter. What does is the catbar or the broom handle or hi-lift jack or whatever gets used first on the tall guy's gut, then on his bowed back, then on the base of his slick bald skull. My father holds the child too long, long enough that his truck coughs out, long enough that when the mother takes the snubnose from the bald man's waistband my father shakes his head no, takes it from her, walks into the store with it by his thigh because he needs gas, he needs chips, bean dip, mustard, he needs everything but to point the gun at the girl behind the register, who doesn't know to tell my dad about the triggerpull, which is in ounces not pounds. He doesn't mean to shoot; he tells her he's sorry, he's sorry, oh God, but she's spread so thin he doesn't know where to talk anymore and he has to leave his chips on the formica, just take the gas nine years down the road with him, into what's becoming night already, his headlights making that center stripe incandescent until it's blotted out by a livestock trailer, its guts spilled all over the sticky asphalt.

What it's left are horses, blowing steam and pain, ears and forelocks burned off. My father rises from the cab of his truck like the angel of death he thinks he is, and when he doesn't have a sickle just uses an implement from the bed of his truck. It's a knife from the knifing rig, the blade thirty-six inches long.

It leaves a line welling in his hand as he walks among the horses, touching each one between the eyes before bringing it down, before bringing them all down, even the mare who gets up and runs from him into the shiny grass, into the fence the same color as the sky. He says something as he opens her throat but it doesn't matter, because he's already miles and years ahead, in a truck stop nursing a coffee, the only thing his liver will allow anymore. His hands still shake around the ridge of scar tissue, though, until he thumbs some dull change onto the table, floats over to the gift bar with the other truckers, all the guilt toys there under the glass, lidless, smiling.

He paces before the counter, drawing close then backing away until he buys them all, all he can carry, and stumbles out the door trailing fuzzy green flesh—elephants ostriches snakes—the waitress picking them up for him. He watches her, waits for her, and in a moment of unexpected tenderness they draw together in the halflight, sway with the padded animals at their feet, the quilted steel blanket of the backdoors of a cross country trailer framing them, her whispering into his neck nothing about love or chance or me, just something about a job, a construction site where he eventually pulls pension pay, where one day at lunch when we've been shoring up the foundation with plywood and two by fours and rebar that'll never have to see the harsh light of day again he blows a casual blue line of smoke and smiles at a dog winding through the scrap metal and slag towards us, towards our food, her teats dragging a thin line of milk. The first bite my father throws just past our feet, and one of the old time hardhats who's seen it all twice already nods, but I don't get it yet, have to wait for the next throw, farther out, then the next, on the lip of the pit we'll pour the cement in, then the next, in the pit. The dog follows. The old-timer laughs, calls for the crusted chute already, it's time—*time*—but for me there's something between me and that dog, like I can't quite reach it, like it's under smudged glass in a truck stop and my father hasn't given it to me yet like I want him to, like he should have, like he did years later when I was too old, or not young enough anymore, and even if he thinks the girl he's dancing with is the one he shot nine years ago, she isn't, can't be, and I'm not that baby the tall man was holding, all the blue snakes on his arm coiling towards me, but still, God, still, maybe?

At the construction site I'm the last one with a crust of bread, and all the hardhats are waiting to induct me, wanting to induct me, and long after I've dropped the crust into the pit along with everything else, I won't stand on concrete if I can help it, even when it's the concrete around my father's grave, long after he's wasted away driving the backroads, looking for overturned stock trailers to redeem himself with. But there is no redemption, nothing you can do. It's like the rabbits we used to put in the cotton trailers with the dog, how they'd run in beautiful, intense circles, faster and faster, until the side of the trailer was the ground for them and everything was skewed, smearing by, and their padded feet were just barely wide enough not to slip through the wire. If we were good people we'd have killed the rabbits, I guess, but then we'd have to kill the dogs too, and you can't go on like that, not for long, not for more than two or three generations, anyway, and then you'll see that sorrel horse standing in the wet grass of the bar ditch one night, her skin jumping in folds, and it won't matter what you say to get on her back, but it does, because she's the one that can take you pounding back into it all over again, if you can just catch her.

BULLETPROOF

for Asael

When Ton and Ricky and the rest of them came to shoot my brother in the street in front of our house, I was eleven years old. My brother took the first shot in the chest, and the second too, and then stood up all the way and walked into the rest of them, like they didn't matter to him, like they weren't going to be enough. He was a rag doll, though. His shirt jumped in spurts from his body, so that my index finger dropped from my right fist, into the shape of a gun, and I looked after Ton's car, and then the day swelled up, the only sound the sound a balloon would make if you were inside it, somebody blowing it up. The houses and streets stretched out like a cartoon around me, then slammed back down tight, to a point. To my brother, his cheek on the asphalt. He'd been looking back to the yard. Later, the paramedic with his hat on backwards would count sixteen bullet holes in the front of his body, would tell my mother how any one of them would have killed him, and my mother, she would laugh, shake her head, because she knew that a sharp, rusty bottle cap underfoot could have killed him just the same, or the steering column of a primered LeMans, or a hundred other things. Already her two oldest sons were dead. She'd been thinking about them earlier, even, before Ton and Ricky and their lowslung Impala. She'd been thinking about them from her side of the screen door, while my not-shot-sixteen-times-yet brother adjusted the stereo he'd just wired into his car, and turned it up for me. I'd moved my head back and forth and he smiled, took me by the shoulders so I faced him, and started dancing the way he danced, the way our two oldest brothers were supposed to have danced. They'd learned it down at the Center, when Lou still taught boxing. You could still see it in the way my brother's shoulders moved, like he was feinting and jabbing, but smiling too, his feet light, tracing important patterns onto the sidewalk. I looked back to my mother to see if it was all right and that was when I knew what she was thinking. She had the side of her fist to her mouth, and wasn't looking away. Later, if there had been a later that day, she probably would have told me that I moved just like one of them, Gabe or Odale, and then she would have pulled me too close to her, until I lied that she was hurting me, come off it already. When what I really meant was that I was eleven. That I couldn't let my still-alive brother see me being a kid like this. But that night, instead, the whole family was over drinking, counting to sixteen on their own chests and then gone in a line of purple-dot taillights, to find Ton and Ricky, or at least an Impala. My mother didn't stop them either, just me, her hands on my shoulders, both of us watching out the screen door. After a few minutes of nothing, I pulled away from her, walked back to the bedroom that was just mine now, and grew up for four years, into all the clothes my brother had left in the closet. I put them on like a ceremony, wore them like a badge, and kept my lips thin and serious. One night one of my uncles talked to me in the backyard about how I didn't have to be like the rest of them, how I was charmed, the last of four. All his sisters had left. I gave him back the same obvious shrug I'd seen him give the guys down at the store, the shrug that was a dare, really, my hands still in my pockets, and he shook his head, looked out across the warped roofs of all the houses. People say he looks just like my dad, but I know it's a lie. Later that week he got picked up, tried resisting, had to go to the hospital, and his wife, the white girl Leeny, nobody knew what happened to her. Maybe she went with one of the cops, even, or had been the one who called them in the first place. His kids, though, my little cousins with the sandy hair, they had to come live with us. There were four of them. In the living room they crawled all over me and I wrestled them and the days passed, became other days, and then Leeny showed back up in my uncle's Grand Prix. She was there for the kids. It was sometime after midnight. I just stared at her through the screen, and then my mother pulled me back, stepped out onto the porch, pulled the door shut behind her. The next morning, the Grand Prix was still there. I walked around it almost until lunch, appraising it, imagining it with different rims, less obvious chrome. Me behind the wheel. Well, my mother said, just suddenly there, biting back her smile, What do you think already? Shining there in her hand, the keys. I asked about my uncle but she just shook her head no, her eyes unfocused. I nodded, understood: he wasn't coming back, wouldn't need a car inside. For the rest of the afternoon I polished the Grand Prix, got to know it, and then, right when it was getting dark, I finally put the key in the ignition, rolled it back to the radio. My uncle's rancheria shit seeped up out of the dash and I smiled, looked into the rearview. Behind me, every-thing was red. I was pushing the brake. I let it off, closed my eyes: my brother wasn't back there. But still, I pushed the brakes again, made myself look, then walked back around to where he'd been standing that day, and tracked the memory of Ton's Impala, sloshing around the corner, all the guns of the front seat leaving paisley lines of smoke up near the headliner. My right hand made into a fist, and then I looked back to the front yard. My oldest little cousin was there, escaped from the house. Running to his dad's car, maybe. I nodded to him that he was cool, that it was all right, I was out here, and then looked back to the street, and felt a thing rising in my throat that I didn't want. I couldn't swallow it back down, though, couldn't look away: the line of fire from Ton's rolling Impala, it went through me, stopped at my little cousin, and then that sound was there again, like the air in a balloon, and my brother was staring hard into the Impala, locking eyes with Ricky, daring him to do it again, even if that first bullet had already killed him, like the paramedic said. It didn't matter. My brother had walked anyway, towards the Impala, *into* the bullets. Meaning Ricky and the rest would have been sweeping their guns back that way. On the low cinderblock wall of our neighbor's house then, I saw what I should have seen that day: two little chips, where two bullets had flaked up the brick. The fence, instead of me. I pulled my top lip into my mouth, looked back to my little cousin in the yard, and nodded, reached in through the passenger side of the Grand Prix for a better station, and, as the light failed all around us, I got down on my knees and moved my shoulders back and forth for him smooth and hunched like a golden gloves, so he could learn too how to dance, and when he closed his eyes to let the music pour through him, I looked back to the street, for my brother, his cheek to the asphalt, his face angled to see if he'd done it, if he'd walked far enough, if he'd saved me.

He had.

SPEAR FATHER

for Kinsey, remember?

HER: Dad, you do not need that spear.
ME: But what if I do?
HER: What would you even do with a spear?
ME: Spear things.
HER: What things?
ME: Things that need spearing.
HER: DAD!
ME: What about zombies?
HER: You'll hurt yourself.
ME: I'll hold it by the end that's not dangerous. That's how you
    use a spear.
HER: I don't think spears are exactly legal.
ME: Not the way I'll use them.
HER: What does that even mean?
ME: It'll be illegal how good I am with a spear.
HER: Have you ever even thrown a—a javelin?
ME: They're different.
HER: They're the same.
ME: Spears are COOL.
HER: Just because you saw one on TV?

ME: That just reminded me. Made me remember.

HER: That you're a spear person

ME: I could be. I am.

HER: Can we unpause the show now?

ME: I could teach you how to hunt with one, I mean.

HER: That would great. That would be wonderful. Thank you.

ME: They're good for if—the apocalypse.

HER: What will we hunt?

ME: Spearable things. You know.

HER: Can't wait.

ME: Do you think they have wood or metal shafts?

HER: We're still talking about this?

ME: Survival.

HER: If we're just gonna—

ME: They're also good for self-defense.

HER: In the apocalypse.

ME: Whenever.

HER: Whenever you happen to be carrying a spear, yeah.

ME: Which should be all the time.

HER: Are they good for ending conversations you don't want to be in?

ME: 'Is a conversation a spearable thing,' hm. I think so, yeah. Why?

HER: No reason. In case somebody in the apocalypse pauses the show and won't stop talking.

ME: You really think there'll be electricity then?

HER: As long as there's spears, I don't care.

ME: Exactly.

EMPLOYMENT HISTORY

In my time I've been an alligator wrestler, a kangaroo boxer, a steer wrestler. A butcher, a baker, a candlestick maker. I once had a job naming racehorses. Another time I volunteered to give suppositories to wild animals. I was giving back to the community; I was Jim Fowler for the day. Old men narrated each of my movements and grinned displeasure through mustaches as thick as buffalo grass. Their eyes were so kind.

Do you need someone who can reach in a pregnant cow and pull out whatever species you say? Husbandry, too, I know it. Sterile mules tremble with desire after I talk to them, my lips brushing the long hairs of their inner ear. I once even got two female emus to mate. The bigger one wore a strap-on, the smaller a liberal amount of mascara it took all morning to apply. The eggs were bloodless and pure.

If you need references, too, please, call my brother, ask him about the frogs' mouths he used to line with firecrackers as a child, or call Bill at Possum Kingdom, ask him how many cats will fit in a fifty-five gallon drum, and whether it'll float, and make him tell you the truth. Ask him if those paper nests that wasps leave in trees look like hanging fruit in the leaflessness of December, and if a person can live off that, and, if so, how long?

He knows those answers. I do too. And more.

A shod horse on asphalt will never stop running.

Cows like to stand facing the wind.

A goat can jump farther than you think.

When black widows are born, they spin a gossamer kite, ride all around the room, disperse. Hundreds of them. You can breathe them in if you want. You have to find them, though, then wait for the fibrous eggs to bloom. Some people probably use straws but I prefer the baleen method: pacing the floor with eyes shut, lips parted in a smile so deep it's hard not to cry.

A horse on asphalt will never stop running, will kill itself under you. I can show you that horse, that blacktop. The sparks that rise from the horse's hooves at night are like nothing else, I promise you. Call me. I'll be sitting on my brother's porch, his cigarettes lined in my mouth like a pagan flute. There will be stars falling in the steaming grass and bats approaching them on wingtips unaccustomed to the earth, and your call, your call will break the silence for me, please.

ABDUCTED

Every time Donald saw a UFO, he got an erection. The problem, of course, was that UFOs didn't seem to be quite as common a phenomenon as they'd been in his youth. Dr. Collins smiled politely, in appreciation, and studied the holes in the tops of his loafers.

"So what you need then . . ." Dr. Collins said, narrowing his eyes to keep up, to record all this for his wife, "what you need is some way of bringing the aliens back, yes?"

Donald didn't have to look away to answer. There was never any eye contact during the examinations. Dr. Collins had given up on that years ago; it was why he'd had the large window cut into the room—to give his patients trees to study, birds, squirrels, life. Anything but the fourteen-thousand dollar chair in the corner, the tile around it splashed with iodine.

"Maybe if they could just do a flyby once a week or something," Donald said, smiling. "Flash their lights a little for the wife, y'know?"

The wife.

Dr. Collins filed that one away too, crossed the floor to the side counter, for the prescription tablet he had to keep locked in the drawer now. The reason for Donald's visit, according to the chart he'd filled out in the waiting room, was prostate, which he'd spelled *prostrate*. It meant to throw oneself facedown on the ground in humility.

Without looking up from his tablet, Dr. Collins asked, "Is that all you need, then? Some more, um . . . close encounters?"

"You can arrange them?" Donald said, his voice rising, incredulous, his hands gripping the lips of the examination table to either side of his legs.

Dr. Collins signed his name with a flourish, letting the s trail out longer than usual—a comet tail, he thought—and shrugged for Donald, said, "You still have to provide the candles and wine, I guess."

Donald laughed with him, and for a moment they were just two gentlemen from different generations, each raised well enough to know how to discuss delicate subject matter. The way Dr. Collins would tell it to his wife, he knew, would involve some of the things he should have said, about *implants*, maybe, about how the *discs* they were both talking about were essentially the same, it was just a matter of scale, of provenance: one came glittering down from the sky, the other across the counter of a pharmacy.

But then Donald stepped down, took the prescription Dr. Collins was offering.

He looked from it up to Dr. Collins, then out the window again.

"I assure you—" Dr. Collins started, trying not to smile.

Donald didn't let him finish, interrupted not so much with words but by centering Dr. Collins in his old man eyes, his face still angled slightly away, as if he were embarrassed.

"I think you maybe misunderstand, Doc," he said, still picking through his words in a way that Dr. Collins could tell there were a lot not being said. "I didn't get excited about the UFOs myself, see. No, no. They never were much but a bother to me, with what they did to the corn and all."

Now he was handing the prescription back.

Dr. Collins looked at it between them like it was an artifact from another planet, and from it up to Donald, just as alien now.

"Then . . . *what*?" he said, not sure if he should be ready to smile or not.

Donald shrugged, rubbed his rough chin with the side of his hand in a way that Dr. Collins couldn't tell if it was the hand itching or the chin.

"The wife, I mean, y'know?" he said finally, looking outside now, but up, too. Dr. Collins looked with him.

"Every time they buzzed our house back then, me, I'd go for the barn, to keep the horses from kicking their stall doors out. But the wife, she'd run out *after* them, see? Then come back— God—come back to the porch an hour or two later, corn silk in her hair, spider web trailing off the sleeves of her dress like a shawl, her chest just rising and . . ."

Dr. Collins studied the sky long after Donald was gone, his new prescription not a prescription at all, but a referral, for his prostate. That's what he had really been there for. Dr. Collins didn't tell his wife about that part of it, though. Instead, the next morning, Saturday, he found himself awake in the house earlier than usual. No coffee in the air, no cars outside. Just dawn, seeping in through the blinds over the kitchen window in beams that, for a moment, seemed to be feeling, scanning. Cataloging.

Dr. Collins—*Stan* on the weekends—walked through the beams to the front door, and out onto the different world of the porch, the automatic sprinklers flowing up into silvery mushrooms, the whole landscape of the neighborhood suddenly, basically, unfamiliar, so that, until his wife came gasping up from the street, her morning run complete, he knew he believed.

"Getting too old for this," his wife said when she could, her hands made into fists around the knees of her sweatpants, her lungs trying to wring all the oxygen they could from Earth's thin atmosphere, and Dr. Collins shook his head no about that. She wasn't.

DAY 522

Because this isn't the movies, the officer tells us that he isn't going to stay up for three days straight, living on whiskey and cigarettes, to find out who broke in through our balcony, nor is he going to troll the back alleys and smoky poolrooms and strip joints for our twenty-seven inch TV, and, as for his shady contacts in the underworld, the chummy, criminal informants he extorts the inside track from when all else is failing, he's probably not going to be calling them either. Nor is he going to get in a loud standoff with his retiring captain about our case, and the chances of him slapping his badge and gun down on any table in the bullpen, well. No. And forget about the forensic crew, unless—unless of course something more's happened here than just a television set being transmuted into crack?

Cheryl shrugs, toes the carpet.

"He did let the cat out," I mumble, and then Cheryl contributes: "We *think* it was the burglar anyway," her arms crossed because this is all my fault. "The 'burglar?'" I ask. "You mean the guy who—" "*The person,*" she cuts in, offended in the complicated, usual way. "The one who, you know, 'burgled' us, then, allegedly, because neither of us would ever do it, carelessly leave the door open?"

"Of course if there *had* been a homicide," he smiles instead, working his badge up, cupping it in his hand like he's ready to slap his career down, stake it all on justice this time, the system be damned. But it's a joke, of course. The punch line's in how he's darting his eyes back and forth from Cheryl to me, murder in our eyes, but because this still isn't a movie, and is pretty much refusing to be, he doesn't fall into some wisecracking referee role for us, and we don't say anything properly witty after he's gone, just sit on the couch like the people we are, waiting to see who's going to apologize first, and for what, staring the whole time into the new twenty-seven inch hole in our living room. Waiting for the cat to come back, though, if it's smart, well.

It's probably just going to be the two of us for a while.

THINGS I'M NOT SO SURE ABOUT RIGHT NOW

1.) Whether our waiter's washed his hands or not

2.) Whether I care

3.) Whether this would matter more or less if my waiter were a waitress

4.) If wondering that makes me a bad person somehow

5.) Whether my wife across the table can somehow see this list happening in my head

6.) Whether or not she's making her own list right now too, now that our waiter's walking away again

7.) If she's got any aprons at home we could use, later

8.) Whether it's asking her that might make me a bad person or if it's not telling her why I'm asking that would make me a bad person

9.) If I'll even care much, during

10.)If she won't be in the restaurant kitchen herself, I mean, in her head

11.)Whether that would make it better, worse, or just fair

12.)If we should both just keep our eyes closed, maybe, wait for our food, and know that if the waiter hasn't washed his hands, we'd rather not know

REUNION

Freestyle swimming in the ocean, lost, just waiting for the sharks to become aware of me in their hungry way, I bumped into Lacy, my old nemesis from high school. She was laid out on an inflatable lounger, smelled like tanning oil—coconut, I was pretty sure, but with a touch of iodine in it, because she always was a cheater.

"Carol *Anne*," she said, sitting up to lower her Jackie O sunglasses, settle me in her not-really-excited-but-very-polite gaze.

There was nobody for hundreds of miles in any direction, but she still had her bikini top tied on.

Her plastic poolware cup in its cushion armrest was empty. It was the first place I looked.

"Lacy," I said, clumping my arms onto the flat part of her lounger, my breath ragged.

She scooched her legs over from my uninvited wetness.

My heart was still going stroke-stroke, *breathe*; stroke-stroke, *breathe.*

"Hot enough for you?" she said, sipping at her straw, her black shades drawn over her eyes again.

I looked past her coppery smooth legs at the horizon. It was always the same distance away.

Below us swam every kind of toothed beast that had ever existed.

Up top it was calm, though. The sun pressing its heat down onto us. *Into* one of us, I guess.

"Rodge likes tan lines," Lacy said, shrugging like what can you do, thumbing one of her bikini straps away from her shoulder. Under that hollow round string it was white, cool, untouched. "Glen?" she added, letting the strap pop back down. Looking at me importantly, like we were sharing here. Like that's what we were doing, yes.

"Glen," I said, as if trying to track the name. Scissoring my legs to keep my chest pressed into the lounger.

"I thought—" Lacy said, biting her lower lip in the most insincere, irreproachable way.

"He would probably like tan lines, yeah," I said, looking behind me, to where I'd come from. If my treading water hadn't turned us around.

We were juniors, again. All over again.

"Eek," Lacy said, sucking air through her straw again.

Soon the brutal UV rays would crack that plastic. I wondered whose breath was in the lounger. I felt my hair frizzing up, felt my tear ducts rimmed with sea salt.

I opened my mouth, felt the words gathering in my throat, on the back of my tongue: that I had to get to World History, to horrible Miss Mack; that I had to print something in the lab before lunch; that I forgot something in my locker.

That I had to get out of this conversation.

It was fifteen years too late, though.

Because it was the only distraction, I studied the sound Lacy's poolware margarita schooner was making, squeaking back into its place.

Maybe fifty yards past it, a ghost sliced up from the glass surface of the water.

A ragged blue triangle, already ducking down into the depths.

Dorsal fin. One you could have projected a slideshow on if it was dark. And soon enough it would be.

"What?" Lacy said, pushing up to an elbow to see behind her.

"Nothing," I told her, and pulled my cracked lower lip in, sucked at the blood I'd been making myself swallow. The blood I'd been hiding all morning.

"You good?" I said to her, pushing away, my arms feeling for traction in the water.

"Golden," she said, luxuriating her tan arms out before her, flexing her perfect nails.

"Well then," I said, and leaned over, spit my blood into the water right beside her, and kicked backwards for maybe ten feet, the way you do when you've just dropped into the pool, are lazing through your first lap, and then I rolled over, pulled my slick self ahead like a seal.

One that was leaving all of this behind, at last.

Stroke-stroke, *breathe*; stroke-stroke, *breathe*.

Stroke-stroke, smile.

LEFTOVERS

The first thing I did in the post-apocalypse was tear my rearview mirror off. Because who was going to be coming up behind me? And so what if I backed into something? And I didn't even wear lipstick anymore. The next thing I did was upgrade to a better car, and then rip the rearview mirror out of that one, too. Those next few months, you could have found me by tracking all the rearview mirrors I dropped out the window. It became more of a principle than anything else. A ritual. Each time I did it, it told me that I was here, that the world had fallen apart, that the old rules didn't hold. It started feeling like a liberation. It ended up feeling like I was crumbling my old life between my fingers, letting it fall away behind me. That was about when I started collecting things. Not rearview mirrors, but the clutter we'd used to have that we didn't absolutely *need* to survive. In a crashed-in carwash I found a team-mascot keychain that broke my heart. At a Mexican food place there was a remote control with "bar" written on the masking tape keeping the battery case on. I took the batteries out, for if they leaked and ruined everything all over again. In a house I had decided to live in for the winter there was shaving cream and a razor. I shaved my legs for an hour, until I was crying. Twice I saw other people. The first man I watched for half a day. He was carrying armfuls of cans from one doorway to another. His boots didn't match. The left was brown and tall, the right was a different brown, but short and with laces. I waved to him once but my hand was below the level of the fence I was crouched behind. I told him I loved him, and then crept away. The second person I saw was standing on the top of a five-story office building, the tails of her dramatic coat whipping around her legs. A scarf was tied around her head. When she stepped off that ledge I looked away. Two days later I had a scarf tied around my head, though. Scarves are the proper headwear for the post-apocalypse. Once or twice I've felt *I* was being watched. Feeling that, I tried to model my headgear in such a way that it showcased its utility, its ease, its permanence if you tied it right. Last week in the top compartment of a stroller in the ditch I found a disposable camera with twelve shots left. What I wanted to see was who was on the first twelve shots. What was on those first twelve exposures. It was the old world, undeveloped, waiting. I wrapped the camera in a chain of light blue latex gloves I'd been carrying around. They were from a shelf of hair-dye kits. Soon, I know, I'm going to unwrap that camera, ratchet its little wheel a few clicks to the left, and I'm going to aim it out at a building, or a house, or a parking lot, and then I'm going to leave it under a shelf of rock higher than the water gets, and when it's found someday, the person looking at that print will see that building or home or those two or three leftover cars like I did, and in that way we'll keep on living, in that way we'll never die.

THE HYPOCRITE

My dad, whose mom was sixteen when she had him, who got my mom pregnant with me her junior year, my dad, his forearm under my chin hard, so I can't get out of the corner of the garage, his face inches from mine, but he doesn't have words anymore. He knows too much. And is already dying the way all fathers die, I think: hope by hope, chance by second chance.

DIRTY SANCHEZ

I decided to break up with him the morning he came down with white flecks of tissue on his face from shaving. It was because he always tried to milk an extra week from his disposable razors. It made him feel like he was getting away with something. But that's not why I decided to break up with him. Not exactly. And it wasn't that little bullseye of red at the center of each fleck of tissue either, even though I knew he'd pinched those corners of tissue from the Kleenex box by the sink upstairs, then left that tissue there wounded, an argument waiting to happen. No, the reason I knew that was about to be our last real morning together, it was that, partway through his heaping bowl of cartoon cereal, he rubbed one of those itchy flecks off, then looked at it there on the pad of his thumb like it was a surprise, like it was a bug, like it was a mystery only he could decode. Because of past discussions, he knew not to set something like that on the kitchen table, because that would just be the first step of forgetting it there for everybody else to deal with. And the trash was all the way over by the refrigerator. So, after another dripping, phosphorescent bite of cereal, he chuckled in his chest like he'd just eureka'd polio or solved some centuries-old math problem, and, like it had been obvious all along, the only real solution, he dribbled that fleck of bloody tissue into his bowl. The milk disappeared it, then his spoon swirled it in, like stirring a memory away. "It came from me anyway, right?" he said, and trailed another bite up to his waiting mouth, to his proud grin, and, me, I looked away from this breakfast. Far, far into the future.

KISS THE CHEF

Before everybody got there, Trace double-dipped a chip in the hot sauce. Because it was his FNA house. And then he did it again, having to cup his hand under the chip so it wouldn't trail sloppy red all over the table.

A few chips later, when Melanie had to run down to the store for more sour cream—the story of their life—he studied a chip he'd pulled up from the bowl, decided it wasn't symmetrical enough, that it wouldn't hold enough sauce, and he dropped it back in, felt around for something better. Like anybody would know, right? By the time the garage door was creaking back up with Melanie's return, all the perfectly triangular chips were gone from the bowl. Onto the broken ones, then.

It was a much messier affair, the hot sauce coating his finger-tips, enough to crust around the edge of his nail, except of course he was sucking them clean. When a broken chip broke off even more, well: in for a penny, he told himself, and dunked his pincer fingers into the sauce up to the second knuckle.

Where they had the chip bowl stationed this time, it was just around the corner from the kitchen, so Melanie was oblivious to all this, was focused solely on the second layer of her famous seven-layer dip. Meaning Trace had no accountability going on.

Because he could, he licked a chip long and slow, then inserted it profanely into the hot sauce, dragged it around the rim.

Hell yeah. This is what being host is all about, he knew.

Was there even any other reason to throw a party?

Before the next part, he called into Melanie, if she needed any help—"thanks, hon, no"—then stepped partway into the living room, to eyeball the sidewalk, the driveway, see if there were any brave earlycomers. Not yet. At which point he realized this was it, his window of time, his bubble of invisibility, his first, last, and most perfect chance. And so he eased back up to the table with his feet slightly wider, unzipped his fly, kind of slid the hot sauce bowl over, and, the name wasn't descriptive at all—this was *cold*—but still, cold or not, he was committed, he could get this done if he could just close his eyes for forty-five solid seconds, close his eyes and his ears, open his mind.

Which is about when he made the spine-straightening discovery that "hot sauce" *was* a descriptive name. It might not burn on the outside, but on the inside it's fire, it's lava, it was hard not to scream and fall back into the wall of the dining room. And then the doorbell did its two long, obscene chimes with that waiting space in the middle, like waiting for the glass hammer to fall, and Melanie poked her head in from the kitchen for the help she'd said she didn't need, looked Trace down then up, then down again, slower. Then back up, for his eyes.

"Who was it who spilled her wine on the couch last time?" she asked.

Trace tunneled back in time to that party, dredged up the name she already knew, had never once forgotten: "Sherry Whitcomb."

Melanie nodded, pulled her blouse down on the sides.

"I'll make sure to direct her to the chips," she said, and hooked her head to the door. "How much more time you need, there, champ?"

Trace closed his eyes, clenched, squinted hard—it was because of that slow, tongue-y way she'd said "champ"—and shook his head no, no time at all. Just a few, more, seconds.

On her way past, to the front door, Melanie brushed her lips across his and trailed her other finger in the hot sauce that said *chunky* on the label, Trace was pretty sure, but was definitely more creamy now.

He pulled a starter chip from the bag, stirred the red and the not-so-red together, and then left the chip there like a little sail, to carry them all into this wondrous night.

A FOOTNOTE ON TICKLING

"Professor, is now a good time?"

"Yes, come in, come in, the captain was just—never mind. You're here about the latest suborbital survey?"

"It's complete. And, Jhresha's initial observations were correct. This species reproduces by tickling."

"Like the extended gestural sparring the Miglodians of Ceta-82 do over the course of multiple solar cycles, you mean?"

"It's much briefer, professor. And more urgent, more improvised."

"With the Miglodians, their sparring reveals the suitability of a potential mate. What does this . . . *tickling* reveal?"

"Nothing, save perhaps if this instance of tickling will lead to a series or lifetime of ticklings?"

"But that's foolish! What kind of biological system would base itself on tickling?"

"It would seem to be the primary mechanism compelling them to proliferate their species. Without the tickling, there would be no new ones born."

"You were probably unaware you were watching a ritual."

"This is already the fourth survey, professor. Tickling is definitely the basis of their reproductive economy."

"Preposterous! If this were really the case, then—then surely it wouldn't be isolated to the dominant species, would it? Go back, observe all the life forms."

"The tickling persists in the majority of them, professor, and in all of the sentient ones. They've even come up with elaborate rites wherein they discuss and strategize and willingly enter into mutual tickling, perhaps as a means of—"

"*Mutual*? Allowing that it's also done in isolation?"

"Multiple times I observed self-tickling, yes."

"Is that even possible?"

"They're a surprisingly resourceful species, professor."

"But if they can reproduce through this self-tickling, then why do they ever tickle each other?"

"Oh, sorry. Self-tickling doesn't actually result in offspring."

"It's just ticking for tickling's sake?"

"Some engage this self-tickling multiple times a day, to the detriment of other necessary survival activities."

"This beggars the imagination, that a species could persist on a reproductive dynamic of *tickling*. For this to work, I'm guessing that the tickling itself must be the goal?"

"Reproduction would seem to be a side-effect of the tickling, yes. One they often try to guard against."

"Then the tickling, which they should be masters of, is instead their master, making them, essentially, puppets of tickling?"

"There are communities and classes who do forego it, it seems."

"Can you imagine it? The Hilo of B6, tickling each other to reproduce? No, we'll bury this laughable species in a footnote in some archive no one will ever access again."

"Yes, yes. Of course."

"Yet you remain."

"It's just . . . after watching so much tickling—"

"No, please don't say it."

"We wanted to understand the fascination, professor."

"You and Jhresha."

"We were just going to try it once."

"Your use of past tense is alarming."

"We can't seem to stop tickling each other, professor. And Jhresha says that self-tickling actually—"

"You do of course realize that shallow engagement in the acts of a lower species such as this can be taken as mockery, don't you? If they ever stop tickling each other long enough to develop spacefaring, then they could someday read through our archives, and take this as an insult?"

"That should be no concern, professor. If they ever stop tickling each other long enough to explore the universe, the species will become fossil. It's a self-governing system they're locked in—quite elegant, really. They either tickle or die."

"Oh, the lengths some species will go to. But at least, if they ever do graduate from this tickling nonsense and become fossil, they wouldn't *then* be locked into these acts of tickling."

"Well, their art does depict these acts in great detail."

"Tickling, graven in stone. What will they think of next?"

"They do seem to like to watch others engaged in tickling."

"They would."

"The deck crew has, um, exhibited the same fascination, professor. That's actually why I'm here, to inform you of that."

"The senior staff are tickling each other?"

"Without fertilizing agents, it's harmless."

"And apparently no longer a footnote. We should quarantine, that's we should do."

"Um, okay. It's just . . ."

"Tell me. No, don't."

"The deck crew has been transmitting their tickling efforts, professor?"

"Then . . . then it's too late already, isn't it? It's begun."

"What's begun?"

"The end, Vyeatt. Soon . . . soon all the ports will have tickling conclaves. Promoters will stage tickle fights and tickle marathons, I don't—wait, is there more?"

"It's just—Jhresha said it would be rude not to invite you."

"Invite me?"

"The deck crew is organizing an instructional session on self-tickling. The captain was supposed to have, um, asked you."

"Yes, yes, I probably should document these last moments, shouldn't I? Just give me a moment, I'll be along shortly."

"Very well, professor. But be prompt. The tickling, by its nature, doesn't last long."

"No, Vyeatt, on that I believe you to be mistaken. It would seem, in fact, that the tickling is forever."

"Do you think the stars tickle each other?"

"To make baby stars?"

"Two bodies in friction will often calve off a smaller mass, professor."

"It was nice, wasn't it? Being sensible, not the plaything of tickling?"

"If you say so, professor. If you need me, I'll be—"

"I know, I know."

"It's just tickling, professor."

"Famous last words."

"You should try it."

"Run along, go ahead and run along, now. Civilization isn't going to end itself, is it?"

NIGHTS LIKE THESE

I brought my orgy with me to the PTO meeting. We were second loudest. Next my orgy came to the grocery store with me, because I was out of milk or butter—something in the dairy department anyway. What I remember best is how cold the refrigerator bins were, at least until my orgy spilled into them. About three in the morning, after a much-needed nap, my orgy hit the sex toy store. Sales went up six-hundred percent. Dawn found my orgy at the early service of the church I used to go to. We gained three members. We tried on clothes at the mall—using my employee discount—and probably stole some stuff on accident, but we left some stuff as well. Then we drank a lot of Gatorade in the parking lot, and introduced ourselves to each other. Two of my orgy were named Stephanie, as it turned out. This was awkward for a bit, but then a van slowed by us very suggestively, and my orgy piled in—safety in numbers—and that van was rocking, creaking, and moaning. The windows were of course tinted, and, after my orgy, thoroughly steamed. One of the Stephanies traced a fingertip heart into that spent breath as we were leaving, and the other Stephanie kissed it in the middle, a little to the left, my brain taking a snapshot of that image—the empty space of her lips—and that's what I remember best about my orgy.

BACKSPLASH

Every time I go back into my mom and dad's kitchen, I stand there in the place it finally happened and I think of my dad, crossing this linoleum floor at night, for his tumbler of whiskey, or I think of my mom, standing exactly there and looking out the window at the morning, and I guess I feel kind of guilty, almost.

I cleaned it all up, though. Of course. Where what happened to Janet happened.

As far as my mom knows, Janet never showed up that weekend. This is also what I told her parents, and the police, and the newspaper reporter. And then her parents, again, over a last dinner.

My dad, though. I don't know about him.

His tools in the garage, I mean, they're all spray-painted around, leaving a them-shaped shadow of peg-board right where they go. Growing up, he always knew if I'd been messing with them, even when they were perfectly back in place.

And the car was the same deal, those few times I actually got Mom to talk him into letting me have the keys. He wouldn't say anything about it the next morning, after my date, but after breakfast he'd always ease out to the carwash, for the industrial vacuum cleaner.

It makes me wonder what I forgot.

You can't bleach everything, after all. At a certain point, that harsh smell starts to be the thing that gets you caught, not whatever it is you're trying to erase.

What I told my mom—loud enough for him to hear, in the next room—was that I'd dropped a glass of cranberry juice in front of the refrigerator, that I always remember the fridge being taller, that the whole house used to be bigger to me. And that I was sorry. But no worries, I'd cleaned it up right after, before the ants could slash their antennae back and forth through the air, taste a new direction to line up.

The cranberry of course was to explain any bits of brain lodged high on the molding under the overhanging lip of the cabinet. Any lingering scream in the air, all these weeks later.

What I imagine is my dad, at nine o'clock, the news winding up in the other room for another spectacular recap of the day's events. What my dad's doing is standing there in his robe and slippers, just using the light bleeding in from the living room to pour his two fingers, neat.

Only, he's not pouring.

He's got his head cocked to the side a touch, like he's remembering something. Like he's hearing back into the past. Like if he squints just right.

And then he looks through the wall of the house and all the way across town, not to Janet's car, probably still trailing bubbles up from the pond, each of them exploding in accusation, but to me. He's looking right at me, halfway across town, also stopped on the way to the counter, as if caught.

We take that next step together, father and son. And the next, and the next, and it's like potato-sack races from his work's old picnics. Except back then it was him, limping us fast for the finish line.

Now it's me who wants to win.

Now it's me who has to.

It would kill Mom if he said anything, of course.

So he tilts his sacred bottle over and he pours, and across town I pour, and we lift our glasses the slightest bit to each other—nothing any surveillance could ever detect—and then we step into all the next rooms of our lives, nobody the wiser, except maybe Janet, but she's not going to be saying anything.

THE BOY WHO CRIED ABOUT WOLVES

This is not a call for censorship. So, if you've find this review through some outlet arguing for tighter controls on content, from watch groups promoting what they call 'decency,' or via some spokesperson decrying the moral decline contemporary cinema's contributing to, then please understand that that's not where my campaign dollars go. Loyal readers will of course know the opposite to be more the case, yes? Am I not the guy who said Rob Zombie's remake of Herschell Gordon Lewis's *Bloodfeast* didn't go far enough? Did I not make the claim that *Nudist Colony Massacre IV* was the true inheritor of Ingmar Bergman's body of work? Have I not circulated my *Cannibal Holocaust* remake petition enough for you to know my tastes? Is this column not called "Video Nasties?"

Still. Come on, people.

Ever since lycanthropy went legit, as they say—or came out of the closet or started baying at the moon or clawing at the door or whining at the foot of the bed or pick-your-euphemism—the parade of transformation sequences we've been subjected to has been almost comical, wouldn't you say? How many ways can human skin bubble and burst?

And, it's not that I don't understand. Used to, even a sub-par transformation sequence would take a day to shoot and cost as much as a used Honda Accord. Now that you can hire somebody to do it on-camera for a couple of cheeseburgers and the promise of work next week, though, all our drama and sitcoms have jumped on the werewolf bandwagon. And the box office—please.

The Girl Who Screamed Wolf has got to be the twentieth movie with that title in the last two years. The only reason it even popped on my radar at all is Gwendolyn X, everybody's favorite maven, one of the few working actors whose tats are real, who can kickstart a motorcycle if she needs to, and who brings her own MPAA rating in with her. Granted, she doesn't always make the best decisions, script-wise, but I'm not going to begrudge somebody for working, for pulling a check.

As for who she's playing opposite this time, well, if his name mattered, I'd put it in parentheses (here). He's a werewolf, that's all that matters. Tall dude, clear-blue eyes, can't seem to keep a shirt on his chest. Before werewolves became a protected species, so to speak, he probably couldn't find work at the carwash. Now his dressing room, it's the same size as the scream queen from *Diva Slumberparty Blues*.

And, this *The Girl Who Screamed Wolf*—remember when that carried with it the parable? When flipping the 'he' to 'she' even suggested a bit of the Cassandra myth, maybe even revealed our own cultural biases?

The studio doesn't remember, either.

Put a 'she' in the title in Hollywood, and the audience expects either eighty-eight minutes of damsel-in-distress or an escalating series of unlikely wet t-shirt contests.

The Girl Who Cried Wolf tries for both at once. Which can work, don't get me wrong. A shelf for everything and everything on its shelf, as they say.

But there comes a time. There comes a limit. Even for this boy.

First, the title doesn't come close to applying. The 'girl' crying wolf in the trailer we all saw, it's not even Gwendolyn X's character Tanya Bateson. It's the neighbor girl, over in the first ten minutes to borrow a box of jello mix. Remember her standing at the door, calling back to Tanya that there's something out there, miss?

Don't feel bad. Five minutes after delivering her line, I'd forgotten her too.

Leaving Tanya Bateson. And *The Girl Who Cried Wolf*'s, ahem, 'story.'

Don't let me pull the rug out from under you here, but it's your typical low-budget home invasion kind of affair: Tanya Bateson is cat-sitting at a friend's house, and, because her friend told her it would look good on her, she uses her friend's hair dye, becoming platinum blond in the first sequence. This turns out to be a bad idea, as now she looks just *like* her friend, whose dangerous ex-boyfriend just got out of prison and's supposed to be lurking around, thus the friend's hasty exit.

You can see where this is going, yes? A handsome stranger at the door, Tanya Bateson unaccountably wearing a read-hooded *cloak* of all things, things escalating in the usual direction for a Gwendolyn X outing: steaming it up in the shower, the music dialed loud enough she can't quite hear the claws on the window, various contrived reflections of her trademark silhouette.

Wash, rinse, repeat for eighty-eight minutes, yes.

What's wrong with this picture, though, what I want to call your attention to, it's that, whereas the spectacle is *supposed* to Gwendolyn X and her questionable clothing decisions—you know what you're getting with her—what actually gets all the camera time, it's the transformations.

Let me lay them out for you:

- there's the one beside the breakfast nook on the side of the house, in the big window behind Tanya Bateson eating French toast with syrup (imagine lots of crosscutting, here)
- there's the one on the roof, by the chimney, with—get this—the full moon-as-backdrop
- there's the partial one in the shed in the backyard, with the kids camping out in the backyard next door listening, of course telling campfire stories
- there's the one right by the mailbox, behind the completely unwitting late-night pizza delivery boy, who, as it turns out, was delivering himself
- there's either another one in the backyard or this is edited-out footage of the first backyard transformation. Either way, there's a cat *and* an owl watching (you can already see their eyes, can't you? never blinking?)
- there's the one in the eventual bedroom the story gets to, with Tanya Bateson tied to a chair so she has to watch
- and then there's the final one, that either gets the animal-rights people up in arms or puts a lump of indignation in the ACLU's throat: this tall dark stranger taking a butcher knife to the stomach and then having to transform to save himself.

And, I'll trust you to guess whether Tanya Bateson's cat-owner friend is the stabber there, and whether she asked Tanya to house-sit as bait, so she could finally get even with her ex-boyfriend.

I'll also leave it to others whether that stabbing-in-the-stomach is latex and a collapsing blade or what the studios are trying to call a 'practical effect,' which is of course code for *If we stabbed him, where's the scar?*

No, what I want you to focus on for just a bit, if you can look away from all the on-line transformation videos, it's the presence of *seven* 'dramatically necessary' transformation sequences in the very limited space of one feature film. Now, taking into account that each sequence (hair, claws, fangs, all that blood, the creaking, the screaming, that thing with the eyes) goes for a healthy eight minutes, that leaves us . . .what? Thirty minutes for *story*? Wait, wait, no: we've got to subtract those pesky end credits. Twenty-*five* minutes for character development and plot, for nuance and particularity, for build-up and resolution, for emotional engagement—for, yes, those things we used to kindasorta *get* for our feature film dollar.

I'm turning into one of *those* film reviewers, yes.

Remember when a solid werewolf film had *one* set-piece transformation sequence? Not necessarily because that's all production could budget in, but because the transformation sequence, it needs to be a spike in the dramatic baseline, doesn't it? It needs to be visual proof that this is real, that this is something we can no longer deny away. It needs to be a point past which the story can't go back, can't be the same as it was.

I'm talking *An American Werewolf in London*, yes. And, no, it doesn't matter even one little bit that it's turned out that particular transformation sequence was real, that they only faked like it was special effects. I'm talking about how it was used in the story. How that transformation was the aberration, the strange attractor if you will, around which the rest of the narrative now had to learn to spin.

In this latest *The Girl Who Screamed Wolf*, though, the transformation sequences, they aren't aberrant at all. Rather, they're the norm.

And, before you raise your hand, Pesky McGee, yes, there's precedent, from the pre-lycanthropy days. 1941, *The Wolf*

Man, when we were asked to thrill and gag at the spectacle of this 'impossible' transformation, when we were asked to peek through our fingers at the *transgression* happening on-screen, at this unnatural mixing of man and animal, Doc Moreau.

Consider that less conditioning of the audience, though. Consider it more representative of our own nature.

In the same way we started fetishizing transformations as soon as special effects would allow them some semblance of the 'real,' so had we, nearly fifty years before, smuggled the camera into the bedroom before even taking its price tag off.

I'm talking our own pornographic tendencies, people. And not the 'uncovering the hidden'-impulse we all probably understand at some level, and possibly champion in certain environments, but the basic narrative structure.

Let me define for moment: pornography is a story where the 'boring parts' are the flimsy excuses that deliver us to the next set-piece, that next—yes—money shot. A visual of that narrative form is the snake who just ate the Seven Dwarves: lump, flat part; lump, flat part; lump, flat part. And we usually fast-forward across those flat parts, yes? Why? Because they don't matter. Because they're not what we're there for. We want the lumps, the bulges, the protuberances.

But those narrative lumps, those dramatic spikes, those choreographed, in-the-contract set-piece money shots, they're not always sex, people. We need to all understand that 'pornography' is format, not content. There's hunting pornography, there's real-estate pornography, there's food porn, disaster porn: whatever gets us to that next delectable dish, well, it's good enough, right? So long as we do definitely *get* that dish, and in the highest resolution possible.

This is how the transformation sequence is being used now, werewolf fans. The stories are no longer pitched as human dramas that escalate and deepen and get recharged when combined with lycanthropy. The stories are no longer dealing with the savage tendencies inherent to this human condition. Now werewolf stories, they're pitched as: we can do one transformation in the kitchen, and one beside the house—the lighting's good there—and one in the backyard, and one on the roof if we do it fast, and can we work my cat in somewhere?

And then when the movie clocks in short—oops—you split one of those transformation sequences in two, get up near that all-important hour-and-a-half mark.

It's an insult to the fans. It's an insult to me.

You know what I want to see? Not a return to pre-lycanthropy times—you can't go back, and I don't harbor shifters any ill will—but what I want is a werewolf movie that hearkens back to when transformation was too expensive, meaning *off*-camera was the default setting. We used to laugh at a character stepping behind a tree in desperation, and some sad-sack German Shepherd trotting out the other side as a scary 'wolf,' didn't we?

But, as cheesy as that was, what it left room for was *story*. For surprise and reversal, for sacrifice and painful decisions. Bubbling skin is great, don't get me wrong. Skin where we have to *imagine* the bubbling, though, it turns out that wasn't so bad either.

I could even stomach those four-foot 'wolves' of yesterday, if I had to. I mean, now that it's out in the open what werewolves really look like, what they can do, wouldn't it be nice to check back in to the fantasy for a couple of hours? Which, maybe that's really the issue, after all. We go to the movies not for the real, but for the fake that *feels* real. Granted, right now we're locked in a cycle of addiction to the all-too-real, to transformation sequence after transformation sequence, like there's any real variation from one to the next, but I have faith, people.

Not in the filmmakers, but in you, the audience. Once we stop giving our dollars to all *The Girl Who Screamed Wolf*s out there, the studios and distributors will have to adapt, will have to—get this—transform before our very eyes, into some new and unguessed-at creature.

Maybe even into a real storytelling industry.

That's a transformation I'd watch over and over.

THE BRIDGE

Celia comes to the bridge on her lunch hour. Everybody from her office has already been. It's a spectacle, a myth, was on the news last night. She has a salad, a clear cup of tea, and forty-two minutes to watch.

By the time she gets there, there's a line of people. They're waiting to tie the bungee cord to their feet or ankles or however they do it, then jump. It's a sport, a distraction for the young, been going on since before she got married to Donald, even, fourteen years ago. But it's different now, since Tuesday. The bridge has made it different.

What happened Tuesday was a man from the office building beside hers, practicing suicide maybe, paid his twenty dollars to the bungee people then did it, stood on the little ledge, held his arms out to the side like flying, and jumped.

The bungee cord uncoiled behind him, thick and blue, and he fell headfirst, eyes shut, then jerked to a stop a hundred feet below.

When the bungee people reeled him back up, he was unconscious; this was why he'd signed their form—because of aneurysm, a loose neck, a hundred other things.

Only one had happened to him, though: he woke in an ambulance, unaware who he was. On the couch in front of the news,

Celia had muted the television and explained it to Donald, that all the blood in the jumper's body had rushed into his head at once, washing away who he used to be. The big reset button.

Donald had nodded to the set. To turn it back up.

Even though the man didn't know his own name, his insurance company did, and was writing him impossible checks for what their policy was calling a catastrophe, a life event. He was set for the next ten, twenty years. Whoever he was, or was becoming, or had always meant to be. This was the lottery.

By Thursday, then, the day after that first broadcast, the line was forming, the cameras rolling, the bungee people refusing to let the city inspect its bungee cord for elasticity. Their argument was that cutting the outer sheath to see the inner would compromise the cord permanently. Really, it was just that that the blue cord was magic, was the one everybody was paying extra for.

Celia had smiled, hearing that, and promised herself to go down there the next afternoon, see the historical event first hand, be part of it. So now, a Monday, she eats her salad and sets her tea on the steel rail of the bridge and tries to take a picture of this scene, this madness, for Donald. All the men and women paying twenty dollars for the chance of starting over as someone else. Playing unconscious after the jump, even. Pretending to be groggy on the particulars.

Already there was an ambulance standing by, the paramedics leaning on their large bumper, their forearms crossed on their knees, sunglasses impenetrable.

Celia looks to her watch—twenty-eight minutes—then back to her building, and the smaller one beside it, and then lunges for her tea when it gets nudged off on accident by a man in a jacket. The tea tumbles into space. Down the rail, a woman looks up from it to Celia, doesn't approve.

One of those environmental types, Celia hears herself telling Donald, later, and smiles, shoulders through the crowd, her salad fork rising to her mouth again and again, and then realizes that she hasn't just been *watching,* she's been in line: there were so many people that they were wrapped up one side of the bridge, down another. Snaking up and down the sidewalk.

This is even better than the falling tea. Donald will smile behind his hand like he does, that his wife was down at the bridge with the crazy people. Standing in line to swan dive off. Maybe she'll even be on the news, but which one? She pictures Donald, cycling through all three stations for thirty minutes, her leaned forward beside him, her hand on his knee, eyes hot from not blinking.

It's too much.

She deposits the rest of her salad in the trash, looks one last time to the bungee station at the head of the line, and turns back to her building. And to the one beside it.

This stops her—that the building beside hers is watching her *back,* maybe.

She laughs to herself quietly, won't tell Donald *this,* no, that she's scared of a building, then smiles an embarrassed smile, tries to step out of it, this feeling of being watched, this feeling that everybody up there in the breakroom can see her all the long way down here, but then, suddenly, it's not the building at all.

In the second loop of the line, inching his way forward, his face half-hidden under the brim of his golf hat, is Donald.

Celia starts to reach for him, to tell him he didn't have to come down here, she was going to tell him all about it, but then he shuffles forward another foot, accidentally catches her eye, and they don't have to say anything.

Celia lowers her hand, swallows, and Donald looks away as if he's already jumped.

MARTIN SCORES AGAIN

At dinner at LaDonna's, she comes back from the restroom and the first thing Martin thinks is, Are band-aids waterproof? Because the one on the end of her index finger should be wet, if she washed her hands. But then of course he realizes what's happening between the two of them, that this is a form of intimacy, taking bread from your lover's probably-dirty hands. That it's practically sex, as close as you can come to it in a public place. Martin smiles, seeing all this, then holds their newfound intimacy in his mouth until it swells nearly past swallowing and she has to ask him if he's okay, which he answers yes, yes, her eyes locked on his as he nods so that he knows he's right, knows he can tell her what they're doing here with adhesive bandages, rye bread. For the few seconds it takes him to explain it all, she doesn't look away from him either, just keeps that polite tenseness around her lips, which can become a smile, the kind of pursing only someone who knows her that well can detect, can share. Martin tucks this intimacy away too, for later, which is good and necessary, since, by the time he's punctuated the explanation with a drink from his wineglass, he's already not getting any of the other kind.

WHEN I'M ALONE I COUNT MYSELF

Jon has difficulty with faces. He can remember hair color with no problem, but can rarely describe the exact shade he's remembering, at least not without pointing at that head of hair. And if he can point at that particular hair color, then of course there's no need to describe it.

The world is frail, he knows.

It could fall down at any moment, with any breath.

Whenever it starts to crumble at the edges, just hairline fractures grinning open, that telltale trembling, Jon closes his eyes.

It's safer that way.

If he's not seeing it, it can't really be happening.

This is obvious.

Jon doesn't keep many items in his pockets anymore. He used to, but his fingers were always darting in, checking on them, making the count.

This is acceptable behavior when alone in your apartment, but it can draw attention in public. Standing in line for a sandwich. Waiting for a movie to start. The bus stop.

Jon lives by a whole host of rules. He breaks them every day:

1.) don't look at fenceposts through the windows of moving vehicles

2.) the number of letters a word contains, compared to the number of letters it has when plural, has no bearing on whether the word can be trusted

3.) feet change paces in regular order; there's no need to watch for variation

4.) never sit opposite a brick wall

The last one can be very helpful, though. Brick walls can be traps, prisoners, loops. Brick walls are for lotus-eaters. But don't say that out loud. The same goes for paneling with regular grooves or lines scored into it. And curtains with pleats can be dangerous as well. They look like fenceposts, smearing by.

The name "Jon" has three letters, but it's the acceptable short form for an eight letter name—nine had his parents William and Dorothy given him the H he so needs for the multiples to play out properly.

Jon can make up for that absence, though. He can heap the world over it, cover it, hide it. So long as he pays the strictest attention. So long as he never forgets.

That's hardly an issue, though.

If anything, it's the opposite that's the problem.

FOREIGN CURRENCY

We'd just about given up on ever taking Gemma 5—its planetary defense system used a targeting relay system we couldn't anticipate, and our programs could never crack it with more than a ship or two at a time—but then Philo found a trick in some old history feed: we don't attack them from outside, with strength, we destabilize their economy, watch them crumble from the *inside*.

He got double rations at evening meal, plenty of oats on the back, and then we set to work reconfiguring the materials bay. That's one thing the old science fiction operas got right: matter manipulation—creating something from . . . not *nothing*, but synthetic and organic chaff, anyway. Which, believe me, we had plenty of, after how long it had taken us to even get to Gemma 5.

Our original mission hadn't even been to *come* all this far, but of course, as happens, the war effort was redirecting our efforts, applying us where we could do the most good.

So, after getting assurances that there this had a distinct chance of finally working, which involved projections and a lot else, we fed our chaff into the matter convertor, to come out the other side as Gemma 5's currency. It took a surprising *fourteen* cycles to produce what our economical analysts told us would be a sufficiently destabilizing amount of currency—this was unheard of; it was using resources we could hardly spare. But, we all knew, it would be worth it if it ended the war, wouldn't it?

All that was left once the hold was full of their currency was to deploy it.

Since the Gemmesians knew they could easily blast any one or two of our ships they let slip through their net, they let us through—for sport, we had to assume. For what counts to them as "entertainment."

And, while deployment was as simple as opening the bay doors and letting our counterfeit currency go, for dramatic purposes—to really stick it to them, show them our fighting spirit was yet intact—we attached cute little parachutes to the bundles. The idea was that watching the currency plummet down and land without *quite* bursting (trust the Gemmesians to pick a currency so tricky to carry around) might send them weeping to their domes, spurring a recession, which would lead to the collapse their society, at which point, with them otherwise occupied, we could easily overrun their net.

The silvery parachutes billowing opening against their purple sky would be torturous, too, we knew. They'd be scrambling, trying to catch each one.

Except our calculation were slightly off—we had too much of their currency, it seemed, were going to just have to push some of them out the bay, let them burst where they would, to good effect or no. It was the *un*burst bundles of currency we were pinning all hopes too, though. Once they trickled into the already fragile economy of Gemma 5?

Our simulations predicted total collapse inside of two cycles, if not surrender before. Aware of our superior tactics—aware that we had a devious mind like Philo aboard—what other recourse would they have?

Our small, strictly utilitarian, otherwise undistinguished cargo ship would be responsible for turning the tide of this galactic war. We would be celebrated as heroes. Maybe, in jest, some official would even rain recreations of our fake currency initiative down over our inevitable parade.

It was going to be glorious.

We didn't even ask Philo to go with, under the net. He watched from the deck.

And what he must have seen.

Our scopes can zero in on the facial expression of a single Gemmesian if we want.

I have to imagine Philo wanted.

Even from the bay after we opened it, we could see how frantic the Gemmesians were—*both* sexes (they have only two), which we'd had a few friendly wagers about.

None of us had any idea they could run so fast. Had they ran that fast in battle, out front would never have reached their system.

But you live and you learn.

Or, well. You get conquered and then you *wish* you'd learned, anyway.

This is all history to you, of course. No, Gemma 5 wasn't tactically vital to the war—why else assign a cargo ship, right? But our strategy, "The Philo Maneuver" as it's now called, it's been used over and over since, and not only with currency. It turns out that Gemma 5 was rather unique as pertains to what they assigned the most value—perhaps due to the fact that they don't have replication technology, so have to do it organically?

Let the scientists and theorists hypothesis over all that. It's chaff to us.

What matters is the effect.

And also how quiet it was in the hold, after we released our cargo, our counterfeit currency.

The Gemmesian's preferred currency, that which they priced advice all else, was loud, see? That's something it's hard for the dramatic recreations to effectively render.

Squirmy, too, with a shelf life short enough that you wonder why a thriving society would even elect to make it so important to their everyday functions.

It was, though. Important.

And then we flooded the market.

Every household had not just one or two squirming bundles to care for and raise and protect and educate, but as many as they'd been able to collect on drop day.

In their mythology, I suppose, and perhaps because of a passing resemblance, I've hated that the records refer to us as "The Storks." But, really, it's as good a name for their planetary boogeymen as any.

Their currency, largely suspended by parachute—the rest long splashed into remnants on their walkways and the tops of their buildings—fell writhing and swirling and crying at just below the velocity at which they burst, and when the Gemmesians caught them, they immediately put bottles and spoons and their smooth mammalian breasts into their currency's mouths, keeping as many of them alive as they could, insuring their own destruction.

Such is war, right?

Such is life.

EASY MONEY

All we had to do was record the sound of a wooden bat on a human skull. The second assistant director was paying us two hundred *cash*. Our first real job since getting here. So we went out, splatted a store-bought cantaloupe all over my grandmother's driveway. Then we did it again, with the recorder on. The second assistant director listened, kind of squinted in pre-apology, like trying to get this bad news just right for us, and said he'd give us another shot. For *four* hundred this time: they really needed that sound. So we tried a coconut—it took out my grandmother's windshield, which was pretty spectacular—but the recording sounded hollow. Like a coconut, not a head. We tried a decorative gourd we borrowed from a planter down the street, and a plastic mailbox, and a half-full pony keg, and a lamp that just ended up sounding like glass. Aluminum bats and rebar instead of a Louisville slugger. The single-car garage instead of the driveway, for reverb. Nothing worked. We slunk back to the set, offered the second assistant director his four hundred back, minus one windshield, but he stepped back like the money was infected. What about a dog? he said. Whispered, really, his eyes doing a different squint thing now. We were way out range of the boom mic's furry tails, of course, and left with a crisp six hundred and fifty dollars, walked up and down the sloped concrete halls of the pound, then had to go immediately to the bar to recuperate. Three beers past the four we'd agreed on, then, we had our big eureka moment: the recorder didn't care if the dog was alive or dead, did it? So we trolled the interstate for the rest of the afternoon, came back with a deer, because the skull was closer to the right size. And because the dogs had all been too splatty. And this time—in the garage now, because of neighbors—we made sure the red light of the recorder was on, and the bat was back to 'wood,' and we flipped a coin, closed our eyes, and took the first swing. The *thunk* was so perfect that we did it again, and again, until we had to lock the garage, take showers. The second assistant director listened twice, the same way people in a restaurant will swish wine in their mouths, then he cued it up an incredible third time, a more appreciative listen—we were really going to make it, all our dreams coming true—and he considered, considered, his teeth working at his lip the whole time, and then he offered us a cool thousand. *Each.* For what? we asked, mostly with our eyes. He looked around at the crew still straggling in, kind of shrugged, and said that, for the scene he'd been tasked with, he needed a very, very *particular* sound. If we knew what he meant. When we didn't, he palmed a snapshot our way, with an address written on back, with a hand-drawn map of how to get to that address, and a stack of times that had to be a schedule. We each swallowed, did a mental kind of gulp, I guess, and we asked what kind of movie was this? This made the second assistant director smile, shrug, say in his quiet way that if we could, say, see our way to *misplacing* the recording of this bat-on-skull sound, he could maybe go twenty-five, total. Twenty-five *hundred*, with the implied promise of more sound-work down the road. So we stationed ourselves where the x's on the map said to, and, because we'd been practicing all week, we knew just how hard to make our first swing, and the second, the third and fourth and fifth, and though our second assistant director had been absolutely right about the peculiarity of that wood-bat-on-human-head sound, he hadn't told us anything about her eyes. How they were just like a deer's at the end, looking up to you, understanding not just that you needed the money, but that the sound, that moist, perfect *thunk*, you had accidentally recorded it anyway, were going to be hearing it for days, for years, forever, until, looking back, this would all feel like a movie, and you'd watch it in your head and kind of narrow your eyes in appreciation, because that really was what it sounded like when you caught somebody just at the base of the skull like that. The sound guys were really on that day, you might say. Or you might not.

CODE

The nurse I'll call Candace walks me through the room my father's already dead in, but for machines. We don't look at him of course, wasting away on the bed. Instead she directs me to the different layers of racks stacked with electronic equipment, and instructs me in the use of each like a kindergarten teacher might. "This is the reset button. We wouldn't want to hit that. And this—well. That's for the doctors. They go to school twelve years to know how to push that button." We laugh politely, just loud enough that my father, if he can hear, will, and perhaps know we're not laughing about him. Next she explains the red electrical outlets and the white electrical outlets: the white are for non-essential appliances (her word) like the bed, the lamp, and the red ones, they're "red because they're never dead." She makes me say it back to her, then explains that they have generator back-ups, should the hospital experience any kind of blackout. I nod, accidentally linger on the back of my father's hand, the fist he's making around the call button. Candace saves me, pulls me back, leads me across the room to the coffee maker by the sink. It makes one cup at a time; beside it, in a ceramic bowl, all the different kinds of coffee. Trailing away from it, down to the outlet in the wall, its power cord. Candace, in what I'm to understand is her hushed voice, points out that the coffee maker is a two-prong job, while the socket's rigged for three. "The third's the ground," I recite from some manual or another. Candace touches the top of my arm, impressed, then latches on, pulls me down to confide that she really doesn't understand all that. But she does know that, for some reason, if you happen to unplug the coffee maker, then plug it back not into the top three (two) holes but the bottom, then something in the walls shorts out. Just for this room, and not every time, mind me, but sometimes. I tell her that this won't be a problem—not only will I not be unplugging it, I don't even drink coffee. "Guests," she says, patting my shirt where she was holding my arm, "visitors," and I nod with her, follow her to the intercom panel on the wall. It's just the standard three buttons, with the base of my father's emergency cord plugged in. Candace pulls the line out and then shows me how it needs to be pushed *all* the way in for it to work, see? I nod, then do it myself—one click, to where it looks all the way in, then a second, hidden click. I nod, am glad Candace is here. "Anything else?" I say, and she looks at her watch, then nods, pulls me into the bathroom and closes the door. "Can you hear anything?" she says. I shake my head no. This is what she wants. "But—but he won't . . ." I say, or try to, and she laughs—of course not, of course he won't be in here. "Then what?" I say, mostly with my eyes. For a moment she looks up to me, to tell me I'm missing the punch line here, and then before I can ask she drags me back out to the room, and again, like when I first walked in this morning, all I can see is my father, sinking into the mattress, clutching at it like he knows what's happening here. My first instinct is to reach forward, pull him back out. I even take an accidental step forward, and am about to take another when the heel of Candace's hand finds my sternum somehow. I look down to why she's stopped me: hooked over the toe of my right shoe is the cord for my father's respirator. It's hooked over my shoe because it's duct-taped to the floor at intervals, so that it humps up from the tile like a sea serpent. How I haven't tripped on it already, I can't fathom. "And you don't want to move the bed, either," Candace points out. I follow the cord to one of the wheels (unlocked) of my father's bed, and see the cord's been anchored around it, so that if I were to even *lean* on the bed . . .

I look over to Candace and her lips are prim, proper, but her cheeks are smiling.

"Anything else I should watch for?" I say, and, now that I mention it, yes: the IV line. If it gets unplugged even for half a second, then an air bubble can enter the drip, work its way down the tubing and into my father's bloodstream. At first it'll be nothing—"That's where the oxygen *belongs*, right?"—but when it hits his heart, well.

I'm not supposed to switch any of the lines either, should I get the urge. And, while I can turn off one light or two lights or all three lights, unless I want to blow out the red outlet, I'm never supposed to turn off all three within any ten second period, and then seek refuge in the silence of the bathroom. If I can even get there without tripping on the cords.

I nod okay, yes, thanks, and Candace explains that it's just her job, providing care, answering questions. That she hopes she's been thorough enough for me, that she thinks she's covered everything, everything . . . wait. Silly her. She laughs at herself for having forgotten this. Yes. She knows it's peculiar, possibly, but if at all possible, if I ever choose to visit at night, say, when there's only two security guards for this wing ("*six* floors"), then I need to be careful about ever wearing a light blue hat with any kind of silver or white lettering, like the kind they sell at the gift shop downstairs. It's kind of a tradition for the night shift:

whichever nurse first sees a hat like that, she has to round up the rest of the nurses, and, for the next fifteen minutes, they all have to clean the breakroom, which is all the way down—

Candace is in the hall now, pointing, I can't see to where. I nod anyway.

"Blue hat," I say.

"Silver lettering," she adds. "Or white."

"I don't—I don't even drink coffee," I call after her, and she bats her eyes, says it's just her job to tell me. But the coffee maker's there, should I change my mind.

For the first few days after she's gone I can't even move, feel like there's fishing line tied from every part of my body to every part of the room, but then on the sixth day—the day the antibiotics my father needs for his bedsores push his fever high enough that he goes into convulsions—somebody down at the nurses' station hits a wrong button, reversing our intercom.

The voice is Candace's, I'm pretty sure. She's telling another nurse that, if both of the crash carts for this floor are in use and one of these patients starts coding, then the closest cart is on the third floor, right? All the way in the east wing?

I nod, keep my hands in my pocket, cross the room to the window. The intercom clicks off politely. Behind me, my father's respirator sighs in what I could take for a laugh, if I wanted to. A complicit, mechanical laugh.

I smile with it, with him, and close my eyes, read again the black lettering on the glass case directly across the hall from my father's room, the glass that has, behind it, a sharp, heavy fireman's axe. The words are simply BREAK IN CASE OF EMERGENCY.

You can tell by the dust on the blade of the axe that, in all the years this hospital's been standing, nobody's ever needed that axe bad enough to break the glass.

I won't either.

THE JONESES

My dad was paying close attention when Mr. Rutherford four houses down came home with Boris, the gangliest of all Irish Wolfhounds. Boris was a rescue dog. His backstory could, for all anybody knew, be Russian mafia, or maybe he had been part of a fashion photography for a while. Mr. Rutherford walked Boris each morning at ten on the dot, which was when the Widow Blakely could be counted on to be at her fancy mailbox, because she didn't want to miss a single thing. Seeing the specter of Mr. Rutherford in his ratty robe walking this leggy supernatural creature on a foggy morning, of course she startled back, tripped on the raised brick border of her flower bed, and pirouetted desperately out onto her still-wet lawn, her coffee scalding her upper chest. Which Moira Davidson, self-assigned protector of any and all widows, took enough umbrage to that her husband Theodore showed up later that week not with a bigger dog— there is no dog in the world taller than Boris—but with a stocky Rottweiler with a head like a cinderblock and a particularly checkered past. The Davidsons and Mr. Rutherford, observing a sort of unarticulated detente, neither wanting to acknowledge this arms-race-with-dogs, walked opposite sides of the street, etc. executing neat flip turns at the stop signs at either end, and taking the crosswalk to the other side. At first, Dr. K attempted to ward these two killers and their inevitable bombs from his impeccably manicured lawn with a spray bottle of what was supposed to be mountain lion urine. The scent was rank and, we thought, impenetrable. All the same, one dog or another found its way onto his lawn, left a steaming deposit. Taking this in stride, Dr. K shrugged, acquired an exotic pet license, and came home not with another spray bottle of mountain lion urine, but with the mountain lion itself. Next door to Dr. K was our young newlyweds, the Andersons, who turned out to have enough connections to, later that mountain-lion week, parade a matched pair of hyenas on thick chains up their driveway, and admit them into their home. My dad grumbled about this, possibly because this was no longer an escalation of size or ferocity, but *number*, which he said, was leading either to chaos or the zoo, neither of which he was interested in being a part of. Our French import to the neighborhood, Claude Carbonneau, evidently felt the same way. What he led from the backseat of his American muscle car—on a dogcatcher's pole, of course—was a scraggly rat terrier, foaming at the mouth with what we could all tell had to be rabies. His little dog wouldn't win in a scrap with any of the other pets, but neither would those pets win, n'est pas? This was a new and unexpected tactic—a wildcard no one could have anticipated, but that no one could ignore, either. The Crane Twins from down at the corner took this as permission, as license for what, perhaps, they'd been secretly desiring since moving in: a black mamba. It was a standoff every morning, that long, tense fall: Mr. Rutherford with his lanky aristocrat, neither of them deigning to look either left or right, the Davidsons— though, usually, Moira—with their rippling mercenary on a leash, Dr. K patrolling with that tawny, slinky killer, its green eyes flashing menace, the Andersons hand in hand, a smiling, trotting hyena to either side, both of them slavering for Claude Carbonneau's crazy-eyed, wiry-haired little nuclear deterrent, all of them giving the venomous Crane lawn a wide berth since they raised the cutting plane of their electric lawnmower. Which was when my dad finally waded into this fray, not with an animal, but *as* the animal: ten-ounce defrosted steaks zip-tied to his shins and a semi-automatic pistol in a modular holster at his belt on the right side, concealed carry permit in his shirt pocket, though he was concealing nothing. He was just out for an innocent walk, right? He would have no reason whatsoever to draw his new pistol so long as he wasn't accosted or attacked, right? Which was when my *mom* came home from the pharmacist with pills to start crushing into his dinners, a few of which I saw her palm into her mouth herself, perhaps to make living in this neighborhood feel less intolerable, or at least not quite so persistently fraught. This standoff up and down the block lasted up until the mamba struck Boris on a foreleg and the terrier infected the hyenas, who in turn dispatched the mountain lion with surprisingly little effort, and were chasing the Rottweiler up the sidewalk when it seemed a legitimate threat to my father, and all fifteen rounds in his pistol, at which point everybody went back to fertilizing their lawns and repainting their shutters and bringing home newer and shinier cars, until the Andersons accidentally—they claimed—backed their luxury SUV through their garage door, which left such a fetchingly ugly wound that the Murchestons two doors down upped the ante with their completely flooded basement, garnering sympathy all around. Across the street later that week, the whole front of the Lumbry's home turned up sprayed with the most offensive graffiti. Even after sandblasting efforts, the profanity and slurs could still be either read or remember, we could never quite tell. In short order, then, trees began catching Dutch Elm disease at a frenetic pace, fences started to weather and sag, driveways showed signs of buckling, and, finally, a kitchen fire in our home (my mom's famous tarts) spread to the roof, then to the houses on either side of us, and pretty soon the whole block was a roiling conflagration, a bonfire where every property was burning at equal levels, meaning the winners could only be the biggest losers—those escaping with the absolute least valuables, those the most bereft and emotionally shattered—but perhaps it was the black mamba, slithering away into the gutter, who actually won that particular go-round.

TRUTH IS A BEARDED LADY

My husband has two hearts. He told me. When he was a kid, sideshow people were always lurking around to kidnap him into the carnival. But he got away each time, just barely. If he hadn't, we wouldn't be together right now. But he only tells *me* about his second heart. His other wife thinks he's like everybody else. She thinks he just has one heart, can just love one woman. I know the truth, though. He trusts me with all his secrets. If either of his hearts is bigger, then it's the one he's given me.

ANIMALS I'VE KNOWN

The goose that laid the golden retriever never got caught, because who would expect a retriever, a dog bred to collect waterfowl, to mount one of the birds he'd been trained to deliver? But, too, we all understand, I think. Are all dogs. I mean, for years you hold their long, delicate necks in your mouth, know the weight of their bodies, how it feels when their muscles undulate from tail to beak, but are warned never to taste. Then one day, splashing through the shallows, no gun behind you, one of those birds turns around, presents herself, and what gets you excited isn't the invitation under her tailfeathers there, but the memory of her neck under your teeth, the way her body can quiver in death. And then when it's done, she's so shy about it, preening the way geese will, her head ducking down to the base of her left wing again and again, and for the first time ever your bird spreads her wings to cup the air, and lifts off into the sky, your seed swirling inside her, soon to be wrapped in delicate eggshell, the shame inside it golden like you, like that afternoon, and safe, because she knows better than to ever warm that egg back up. Except in memory.

THE FAMILY THAT READS TOGETHER

As a joke on our dad once we waited until he was asleep then took down all the books in his study and put them back on the shelves backwards, with the spines *in*, facing the wall, and then—this was my sister's idea, not mine—we also arranged them by height, so that the short ones started on the right side of the door then grew taller as you tracked around the room, finally getting to the really big ones on the left side of the door. It was beautiful.

Our dad screamed in agony.

At the time, he had about six thousand books. It had taken us all night. As for how he got us back for this, he composed himself by degrees (it involved straightening his shirt over his chest and licking his lips too much, until they shone) then just pretended not to have noticed what had happened to his study, and, instead of changing all the books back, too, or making us do it, he started living in the walls of our house, so that we only saw him when he darted out for food.

What he was doing in the night, we were pretty sure, was scraping away the backsides of all the walls of his study, so he could see the spines of his books, run his fingers over the raised titles, linger over his collection like he used to before it turned its back on him one morning, and though we staged vigils all through our teens and tried to lure him out with apologies spoken into electrical sockets and pleas whispered into light switches, he had gone too far. Our joke had clicked something over inside him. He didn't see the humor of it at all, and so, in response, isolated himself over the course of years, insulated himself from us with his clandestine studies, leaving us with only two options: either turn all his books back around and arrange them alphabetically, or leave some perfect book in the middle of his study, just on the floor, like all the other books had turned around just now to look at it.

Would either tempt him out, though?

If we turned all his books around, would we find him in the morning pale, gaunt, and panting in his old chair, as if he'd always just been a reflection of that library, or would he fill the walls with another scream, because his inside-out world had just turned even more inside out? And . . . and if we left that lone, perfect book out as bait, for him to retrieve while we were pretending not to look, not to listen, would he find a way to wedge it into his shelves backwards, then return to the walls, start scratching again, making a window there so he could see that title too?

Nevermind that if he scrapes one bit more off the backsides of our walls, the house will surely come crumbling down around us. Unless of course the books have become load-bearing themselves, which is entirely possible, but to accept that we also would have to accept that for all these years living in the walls between our rooms, our dad hasn't been able to read a single page, for fear of bringing the roof down onto us, and if *that* were true, if he loved us more than his precious precious library, then why would he be living in the walls in the first place, right? Better that it all fall down, we say, so we can stand from the rubble, say all of our insincere sorries to each other, and close the book on this whole affair.

SUNSETS UNLIMITED

Riding through the desert I came across a cowboy in the narrow shade of a saguaro. He was doing stomach crunches. I crossed my arms over my saddlehorn and watched him for a few reps but ended up just studying the wavery horizon, as punctuated by his rhythmic breathing. It was hardly labored. I didn't want to interrupt him, of course, but by the time that became an issue I'd been there long enough that to wheel around and continue on my way would be a comment on his hospitality. It would matter little now, but six or nine months down the road he might split a pair of batwing doors in some miner town on the boom, and there I'd be at the bar, and there might be words, or at the very least a prolonged session of averted eyes, culminating in one or the other of us over-imbibing. So, together, in our heads, we counted to fifty by twenty-five, at which point—raising my arm in preparation at sit-up forty-eight—I coughed politely, suggesting neither that I'd been riding drag since Amarillo nor that my water bladder was long since dry. Just that, as was obvious, I was there.

He stopped half way to his knees, his arms butterflied out from the side of his head, and squinted up at the silhouette I had to be for him. So as not to cause any misunderstandings, I rolled my shoulders as if stretching, giving the sunlight opportunity to glint off any badges on my chest, had I been wearing any.

"Yes?" he said, the apparent weariness in his voice transforming me at once into someone who had just recognized him through the plate glass of a barbershop, and now feels compelled to interrupt an otherwise pleasant shave.

I took my hat off, rubbed my stiff sleeve across my forehead.

"That your horse there?" I asked, nodding to it, then made a production of clamping my hat back on.

The cowboy answered by sitting up and purposefully regarding the only other horse in this desert that *could* be his.

And then he pulled that penetrating stare back, settled it on me. Leaned over and spit a teal line into the sand as if clearing his mouth.

"That your'n?" he said, nodding to the mount under me.

I grimaced inside, was prepared to grin displeasure if need be, possibly squint, but fortune was on my side that day: a scorpion chose that exact moment to scuttle across behind the cowboy, in the wallow his sit-ups had carved into the sand.

Without looking over from him I drew and shot, one liquid motion, plugged the scorpion in its tracks.

The cowboy didn't flinch, just gave an amused snort. His arms looped over his knees now, his left hand circling his right, his own holster looped over the Bowie stabbed into the trunk of the saguaro.

"I interrupting you here?" I said, leaning back so as to look down my own chest without my hat giving shade to the single cartridge I had cause to thumb into my cylinder.

"Interrupting me . . ." he said in reply, as if considering its many and diverse meanings.

"I just—" I started, but he wasn't finished yet: "You figured since we're the only two out here, maybe we should hombre up? Chew the fat, as it were?"

Working with a deliberation that had to belie my years, I unwound my neckerchief, used it to dab unnecessarily at the outside corner of my left eye.

"I am interrupting," I told him, nodding in deference if not quite apology, giving my mount signal that we were moving on.

Before I could pocket the neckerchief, however—putting it on in the presence of company has always seemed such an undignified act—the cowboy coughed once, in mock attempt to disguise his laughter.

I cut my eyes back to him.

"I should be insulted," he said, "that you would think me capable of behavior such as that."

Over his shoulder, his horse whinnied, greeting mine.

"Meet all kinds out here," I said back, not deigning yet to relax my face, as this might be a continuance of the ruse— me, dry-gulched by his wit, the vultures above snickering at this outcome, that Bowie-wound in the cactus weeping down through the spines for me.

"That you do," he said, lying back into the sand again, oblivious of the chance of a scorpion stinger buried there.

And so he started again, his workout incomplete, apparently.

For another fifty-count I watched him, and finally had to smile.

His breath was coming with more difficulty now, his spurs occasionally breaking free of the sand, the saguaro's shade dialed past him a slight bit, the minute hand of an immense clock.

"Well," I said to my mount, my hand along the quivering muscle of her neck, and then, with all due surreptitiousness, let my other hand brush my own stomach.

The last boarding house, the fare had been beans, and then more beans, carbohydrate on top of carbohydrate.

"You mind?" I called down to the cowboy, and when he didn't answer I settled into the sand a discrete number of steps away from him, my horse hobbled loosely, and proceeded into my own sets of labored crunches, and in this way we settled into the arduous task of taming this inhospitable land.

MY FINGERS ARE CALLOUSED FROM HANGING OFF CLIFFS

I buried my pregnant evil twin alive the other day, and if the grave was shallow, that was only because, after mounding all the blackmail photos and albums of family secrets and missing files (both ours and the Donovans'), all the dirt wouldn't fit back in the hole. It doesn't matter, though. I'm pretty sure my life is going to be perfect from here on out. At least once I have my operation, so I can secretly marry my now-gay ex and take him for all he's worth. Provided he still has amnesia, of course, and hasn't gone blind or comatose or, heaven forbid, had an operation himself, and assuming that, when he abandoned his evil twin in the woods all those years ago in order to steal his inheritance, that twin died. Otherwise that twin—my son's real father, yes—might find and save *my* twin, and who knows what complicated scheme they might hatch then. Which is precisely why I'm driving so fast right now, on this slippery road: if I can just make it to the Donovans' mansion by dark, and get one of them into bed with me, preferably one I can pretend I've become pregnant with, then I'll have the perfect alibi for the approximate time my twin will be running out of air. Nevermind those cryptic notes I've been getting lately, which are supposed to be from my dead mother but are probably really from my son, who for some reason (probably his stepsister, whom he accidentally dated for a while) has become taken with the idea that death is a temporary thing, a state you can bounce back from after a year or two. He's got a lot to learn, though. Give him a year or two living in disguise with the Donovans, as one of them, and he'll come around. Not that there's no chance that my mother lived through her accident, mind you—we never found the body, after all—but, I mean, if you overdose on designer drugs then slide off this road in the rain like she did, it's not like you could forget who you were and live in a cabin so long that you actually started to look like a whole different person, right? I can imagine it, though, I suppose. Sitting in your chair by the fire one day, then hearing that key in the door that could just be your rustic husband, home with something that looks like firewood at first, yes, but, as it turns out—as it always turns out—the only reason he picked this injured girl up was because that necklace she's wearing, it reminds him of something, of another life he might have led, before *his* accident or brainwashing or trauma or whatever.

It doesn't matter.

If it comes to that, I'll pretend to still be unconscious against his chest, to push my forehead into his rough shirt, because who knows, right? Chances are, if he's not my real father then he's my next husband. Either way, I'll just keep my eyes closed, try to come up with a long-range plan that'll be better than the last one, perfect even, but might require returning to that shallow grave for certain documents. If I can only remember where that grave is, I mean. And if everybody else isn't already looking for it as well.

THESE AMBER WAVES OF GRAIN

Martin liked to stay drunk around his son. As a lesson, an example of what not to do, how not to be. So, the more excessive or irresponsible or plain old criminal his behavior, the better it was for his son. The only real problem with this, aside from fines and health and all that, was that nobody realized what a good parent Martin was, what a sacrifice he was making—not just his liver, but his soul.

Give them time, though, he told himself. In a few years, all his neighbor's kids were going to be in pre-AA mode, their eyes furtive over every Thanksgiving turkey. Martin's son's eyes would be different, then, he knew. More focused, less seething with vague resentment against all adults, brimming over instead with promises not to be an embarrassment like a specific adult. Not to be anything like him at all.

Martin had no doubt it would work, either. After all, the way he'd learned not to yell was by growing up in a loud house, mad people always storming up and down the halls, throwing brushes and ashtrays and, once, the cat, who screamed the whole way through the air too, adding to the din. His son was lucky, really, lucky that Martin's own father had been a strict teetotaler, so that alcohol had an almost mystic, mythic quality for Martin at twelve, at thirteen, and on until the day they finally put his father in the ground, unpickled, twenty years later.

And of course the person who least understood all of this, it wasn't Martin's wife, the boy's mother. Her father had been a conglomerate of five or six different live-in boyfriends. Needless to say, then, her expectations were low—actually, she seemed to be more satisfied with Martin the less he surprised her. Like his behavior just confirmed her suspicions of the world, hardened them into certainties.

No, the person who understood the least, the person who was the least grateful of anybody, that was Martin's son himself. The fights they had in the living room could draw sirens from all over town, which, for Martin, was always a chance for another lesson: you don't want to resist arrest, son, or run from the authorities, either, or smart off, or throw things (the cat), or try to take any of the neighbors hostage with one of those garden hoses with the spray attachment.

Not only will the police not negotiate with you, but, after they've tackled you, they'll sometimes turn your weapon of choice back on you, to sober you up.

These were lessons of irony. During them, Martin would stare at his son, trying to make them take.

When it was all said and done, though, the weekend over, the footage passed around to all the interested parties, another arraignment burning in effigy in the back of Martin's mind, then his son would show him the only affection they both understood: walking up the long concrete hall to sign Martin out again, his footsteps falling for all the world not like a boy's at all, but like the boy's grandfather's. Whose own father must have been a drinking man, if Martin knew anything at all about the true nature of things.

SO THIS IS WHAT IT'S LIKE

When Evelyn stood from the car, she wasn't sure she was seeing what she was seeing.

Her husband's bald head, not just cresting over the tall backyard fence, but *rising*. And rising.

"Terry?" she called out.

He was on the trampoline. The one their son Marty had assembled for his kids when they came over and had energy to burn.

Evelyn started to pull off her sunglasses to get a better look, but stopped at the last moment. She'd just had her eyes dilated and the doctor had warned her to leave the dark wrap-around glasses on for at least an hour.

Technically, she wasn't supposed to have driven home. Most days, she could expect a friendly chiding from Terry, about taking such chances at her age. At their age.

Not today.

Evelyn cautiously took a step toward the fence and whatever this was that was happening. She reached out for the car to steady herself. The metal was hot or her skin was thin. Both.

Terry rose up again, his arms rising to shoulder level and an expression on his face of . . . not amusement. Wonder?

What ever could have possessed him to climb up there?

Instead of going through the house, Evelyn figured out the complicated latch of the gate and stepped gingerly into the backyard. Into this thing that was, apparently, happening.

The springs creaked with Terry's weight, then launched him back up into the sky.

Ever since the grandkids had come up with "air-dodge basketball," the safety netting that had guarded them from falling off the trampoline was now the trampoline's bed skirt.

"You're going to kill yourself!" Evelyn called out, and was surprised to hear her voice crack.

Terry rotated his head around at the top of his jump, trying to find her before gravity snatched him back down.

Creak, launch, hang.

"Ev!" Terry called down, his voice not the kind of steady she was expecting if he was having fun.

"What are you doing?" Evelyn said back. She inched closer to the trampoline.

"I can't—" Terry started, apparently out of breath. Once he'd shot up again, he got out what he was trying to tell her: "Can't stop."

Evelyn tracked his body through the air.

"What do you mean?" She latched onto the trampoline's frame so she wouldn't fall backward, trying to keep him in her field of vision. "Why are you *up* there?"

Her voice wasn't shrieky yet, but it was climbing. It was close.

"Call the—call the—" Terry said in his broken, up-and-down way.

"Fire department?" Evelyn said, her face warming with emergency. "Just stop jumping!"

"I can't!" Terry said back.

Evelyn backed away to try and reassess, to look for some

great hook she could pluck him from the air with, or a lever to slow the trampoline's bounce. Anything.

Terry was right in the center of the black elastic mat. The perfect spot, where the grandkids always tried to get to, to reach the highest, to hang in the air the longest. Evelyn couldn't bear to watch them anymore, now that the safety net wasn't there to catch them. But they were young, she told herself, whenever they were over. Their bones would knit.

Terry's wouldn't.

She could see now that he wasn't voluntarily jumping anymore. Every time he came down, he *had* to flex his knees to absorb some of the fall—to keep his bad knee from going out—and then he was pushing back, to keep from collapsing.

If he tried to stop, he'd slump over and the trampoline would meet him coming up. She'd seen this a hundred times already with the grandkids. He would launch at a crazy angle to the other side of the trampoline, then bounce back the *other* direction. Or he'd get tangled in the springs. Or, she feared, half a foot farther, he'd crash into the frame.

It would break her husband of forty-nine years. It would break him in half.

Evelyn steepled her hands over her mouth.

"Just, just—" she said. But there was nothing.

Terry was trapped.

What could the fire department even do? Tackling him mid-jump would be a disaster. Cutting the trampoline open under him would break his legs, even if they were able to get a pad under there. If they could somehow lean a ladder over the fence, they could pluck him up at the top of his ascent, but she knew his legs wouldn't last.

Evelyn clawed her phone up from her purse anyway.

When the operator answered, asking about the emergency,

Terry grunted and Evelyn dropped the phone into the grass and rushed to the trampoline.

His bad knee. It was going.

"*Terry!*" she said.

He was twenty feet in the sky now, his shirt floating in the air, his eyes wide with uncertainty. His bad knee was pulled up higher than the other, to protect it.

Coming down this time, Terry was fixed on her.

He was calmer now.

No, no, Evelyn shook her head. It wasn't that he was calm. He was *ready*.

This time, *this* jump, one leg was enough. He didn't collapse. But he had to bend deeper, push back harder.

It launched him even higher.

The grandkids would be running around the trampoline with delight, she knew.

Grandpa was going to win. He was going to go higher than everybody.

"You stupid old *fool!*" Evelyn called up to him.

Terry looked down at her like an apology, like he was caught, like what could you do. He was still the same boy he'd been at twenty-two, at thirty-eight, at fifty-five.

He'd had to try, hadn't he?

The trampoline had been there through the window for going on two years. For two years he'd been watching it.

"Go inside," he said to her, out of breath, sinking into the trampoline on one foot, nearly at her level for an instant before rocketing up again.

Evelyn sucked her breath in. That's what he'd told her every time the sheriff's car had pulled up during Marty's high school years. It's what he'd told her when the neighborhood kids had massed at their front door, yelling about what had happened to

Clade, their second dog. It's what he told her that day in their first house, when a funnel descended from the clouds. *Go inside.*

Her chest swelled as she took another deep breath. He didn't want her to see what was about to happen to him.

Evelyn stepped out of her shoes.

Her hands were still wrapped around the edge of the trampoline.

"Wait," she said, tracking him up and down, trying to get the rhythm right. "Wait for me," and the last thing she did before stepping up was peel off the doctor's sunglasses so she could look up into the bright-bright sky and see her husband hanging there, waiting for her.

APPETITE

"Hold on," my uncle said, when I was about to tell him that that was the hamburger stand I was talking about. Hold on, so he could hear the tollfree number at the end of the ad on the radio. It was for male itching. I looked down to the two fingers of his right hand he had to my sternum, keeping me there, quiet, my back against the passenger seat, and, when the ad was over, he let his foot off the accelerator and hooked his chin ahead of us, to the hamburger stand I'd been talking about all day, said "That one?" and I shook my head back and forth just once, no. That we should just keep looking, maybe.

SOLEMN BURGER

Nick had fallen in love once at the Queen. That was the burger joint in Ashmore. He'd been coming there since forever—first with his dad, Francis, then with his own son, Francis as well. This time he was alone though, and hadn't been to the Queen in months. Standing in line, he felt the nostalgia welling up but couldn't identify its source: Francis his father, Francis his son? A way someone had looked at him across all the booths, on the way to a party he should have gone to?

The three girls in front of him in line were home for the summer it looked like. Their earrings and shoes no longer fit Ashmore, anyway. But it hadn't been long for them, either. They were the daughters of the homecoming queens and runners-up from Nick's sixth grade year, probably; he'd watched through the wooden slats in the bleachers as the mothers of these girls circled the track in their dealership cars, then tried to hold his breath until they came back around.

He smiled to himself a bit, inside, didn't even know he still had that night to think about—the way the dust under the bleachers was so fine it settled on his lips, his face.

When the girls stepped forward in line, he stepped forward too, his eyes feeling down the menu, falling through the burgers and chili dogs and shakes and grilled cheeses with jalapenos.

Behind him, he knew without looking, was the heavy playground equipment salvaged from the drive-in. At the drive-in there had been gravel and cigarette butts and pulltabs, a safe distance between the swingset and the merry-go-round. In the fence by the Queen now, planted in plastic grass, the equipment felt cramped. Francis seemed to be able to feel it, even: a lost expansiveness; no backdrop of impossibly tall figures, moving slow and deliberate on-screen.

The burgers they'd eaten that time when Francis was six had been morose burgers. It didn't say that on the menu.

Nick pursed his lips, thought it hard in his head so he would remember it—1:18, he had to be back at 1:18, since Sam had taken an extra quarter hour for lunch—and when he looked down from the menu the three summer girls were looking at him . . . no, *past* him. To the equipment.

Nick scratched his chin on his shoulder, looked too.

It was a boy the girls' age, about, sitting in the swing smoking a cigarette, slitting his eyes up at the sun. He was a kid Nick had been seeing around Ashmore for about three years now, like a shadow. When a green panel truck passed behind him, the line of the kid's exhaled smoke traced a sling in the air, hung there so perfect and impossible.

The three girls weren't watching the smoke, though. And it was their turn to order, anyway. Nick nodded ahead for them, and one of the girls registered him, her eyes flicking behind her like a deer's might.

She touched the side of her hand to the taller girl beside her, and the second girl nodded a suspicious thanks to Nick, and he found himself almost saying a name for her, but then realized he didn't know what it had been going to be.

He was going to get the solemn burger, he decided. The one you stare at and hold, unsure where to start.

But then—it was the third girl.

She had never looked away from the playground.

"Don't," the first girl said to her, hitching her own purse up, a defensive measure it seemed.

Nick looked to her, a new grip in his chest.

She nodded, though, this third girl, nodded as if it were too late already, this had been building for years, and ran her right hand under her shirt, to her left shoulder, shrugging out of her bra.

She was still staring at the boy on the swing.

"Hold this," she said to her friend, pulling her bra from her left sleeve, oblivious to Ashmore, and then walked a straight line out to the story of the playground, in a way that Nick knew she could feel the plastic grass pushing up against the soles of her feet.

He breathed in and held it, waiting for her to come back.

THE UMBRELLA TREE

After the second funeral, Hildy picked her way out to the old tree house. Her big brother JT had built it in 72 when Hildy and Michael had been ten and JT had been home on leave.

The tree had been big then, the biggest they could find, but it was bigger now. Because of the way the crown was shaped, they'd called it the Umbrella Tree, and had stolen a broom from the house to sweep all the leaves and junk out from around it.

The service had been small—there weren't that many of them left, and the ones left didn't live around here anymore. Hardly anybody did. Towns live and towns die. It's the natural progression.

Same with people.

And big brothers.

"I wonder what little Michael looks like now," Hildy's Aunt Glen had asked, sneaking looks at Hildy's sagging features to guess what her twin looked like.

"So do I," Hildy said, and then started when the soldiers fired their rifles, clutching her tissue to her throat.

Michael had started drifting away in their teens, had drifted farther in his twenties, often landing in jail, and in the decades since—

But Hildy wasn't here to dwell on Michael, wherever he was. *If* he was.

This day was for JT.

Their first funeral for him had been in 74, when he was MIA, presumed KIA, which Michael had gotten into fight after fight in the parking lots about, insisting JT was a POW, that he was fighting his way back, that he was going to show up and prove everybody wrong.

But now, two years ago . . . Michael was right, JT *had* made it back. Just, fifty years too late.

There had been some confusion about whether a second folded flag would be offered to Hildy—her mom had kept the first, and who knows where it ended up—but this next one was tucked into itself in the backseat of Hildy's Buick, parked at the pullout where the mailboxes used to be.

Hildy's front door on the passenger side didn't lock, so she was concerned about someone walking away with the flag, but . . . did anyone even use this road anymore?

She didn't think so.

She was surprised to even have remembered the way back to the Umbrella Tree. But ten years old or in her sixties, her feet knew the way. Probably from all the times Michael and her had crept out here by flashlight, so Michael could mumble his prayers for JT, holding onto Hildy's hand because he said that doubled the power, made super sure it would get through the static of all the other prayers going up.

And she should have brought her headscarf for this, she could tell. The clouds were low and heavy. *You're getting ditzy in your dotage, old girl*, she chided herself. But she also liked how cavalier it felt to only worry about getting there, not about whether she would get drenched.

It had rained a lot where JT had been, she knew.

It surprised her that she still remembered him so well. How, instead of easing their dad's truck or the little Farm-All out to the tree with the lumber, he'd hiked it out, balancing planks on his shoulder and assuring them it was lighter than a pack.

He'd held the dull silver nails in his lips, the pounding of his hammer a heartbeat in the afternoon.

"You're not getting *ditzy*," Hildy mumbled to herself, parting some cattails with her hand, "you're getting sentimental."

But she'd earned the right, hadn't she?

The tree house was still there with the tree, too . . . sort of. It was either in the same place, or it was three feet higher, only, it was *her* that was taller. The floor was tilted up, the railing around the platform was overgrown and sagging, but the nails JT had set were still holding it up.

If she pulled them out, set them in *her* mouth—?

But no.

Like she could still even clamber up there. Just her luck to try, snag on something, and be stuck up there.

Hildy nodded, sniffed, and, when the drizzle came on, hissing in the heat, she waited it out by guiding what leaves and twigs and beer bottles she could away from the tree, making it clean and right again.

And then she walked back to the car alone, not letting herself admit that every time she'd peeked up into the wall of rain, she'd been biting her top lip in, waiting for a pair of wide shoulders to be there, limned in a spray of silver.

Sentimental and *ditzy*, she told herself.

Her skirt was damp from the tall grass by the time she stepped back into the ditch, balanced back across the culvert.

There were no headlights coming from either way. Not one of her dad's farm trucks, the mirror and probably even a fender shaking like it was going to come off. Not the Firebird JT had left behind, that Michael had claimed after high school, then, Hildy was pretty sure, sold for a few hundred dollars. Not Aunt Glen, her daughter driving her around like a hired chauffeur.

It was just Hildy.

But as long as she remembered the tree house, it would still be there, wouldn't it? In coming years, she could pull over here in the ditch, know the Umbrella Tree was still out there, and that two ten-year-olds were still going hand over hand up a knotted rope to it, seeing if they could get high enough to see their brother halfway around the world.

She settled down behind the wheel, pulled the belt across her shoulder, and—

Michael was there in the mirror, sitting in the backseat, holding the flag to his chest, his eyes already holding hers. His face was haggard, his hair long and stringy, grey and wet, and he was wearing an old BDU jacket.

Hildy held onto the steering wheel with both hands and looked down at the horn button, because she didn't want to startle him away after all these years.

"Oh, Michael," Hildy said. It was all she could muster.

"I never can get any farther than here," Michael said back, turning to look into the trees, down what had used to be a path.

In response, Hildy stepped out, hauled the back door open.

"We'll go together," she said, brooking no objections, and held her hand out for his and snapped twice for his, never mind that the clouds were pouring again—the Umbrella Tree would keep them dry.

"You look just like him, you know that, right?" Hildy said, leading him across the ditch.

Michael nodded, slow at first then faster, his arms still hugging that flag like it was proof, and they marched out into the trees, the rain washing the years away.

STATES OF GRACE

The lies I tell the mentalist truckdriver who picks me up are ill-conceived and poorly-delivered, but he takes them in rollicking good humor. We push on. Kentucky, Tennessee, the Carolinas; produce, alternators, women's dresses. Sleep comes 10cc at a time. At an all-night diner in Louisville, I make twenty dollars pushing birdshot into the large pores of the back of my hand. They don't resurface, but bead together inside me, stack themselves in my veins so that if I opened my wrist they would well up like a shiny pod of peas. I long for an X-ray and the trucker obliges, hurtling me through the window of his cabover, onto the hood of a parked car already halfway under us.

The X-ray tech follows the stainless steel shot on the film with the painted end of her fingernail and sells the image to the tabloids.

I fall in love with her.

We run away together. Georgia, Florida, Alabama; Freon, crank, lawn fertilizer. At a gas station outside Savannah we eat plastic hamburgers we'll never be able to pay for. They taste so good. The trick I offer the clerk in trade for them is a pencil, balanced on its lead point, progressively larger tubs of butter balanced on the eraser, the world motionless around it, us. The pencil is an intricate part of Georgia's lottery structure, though, and as the clerk's shaking his head no about my offer, the next customer in line lifts a disposable camera off the impulse rack and captures this structure for the local paper. The weight of the flashbulb drives it all down.

"I'm sorry," I tell the clerk, and pass him the note we'd already written with the pencil. The X-ray tech I love raises a pistol reluctantly, lets the hum of the A/C serve as punctuation. Forty-seven dollars richer and wanted on four radio stations, the X-ray tech looks deep into me and asks how this turned out last time, and without missing a breath I lie how the law caught up with us in Arkansas, our Buick's autopilot set for the steel gates of Graceland, and she nods into it, falls asleep.

When she wakes she'll know I made it all up, so instead I leave her with it, step out of the moving Buick just as it coasts under an approaching eighteen-wheeler. In the slow moments before impact the headlights bathe her face, her driverside cheek transparent for an instant, and the truckdriver who saw this coming all along doesn't even bother to lock his arms against the wide steering wheel.

In the aftercrash of glass I arrange myself on the hood and wait for it all to start again, insist hours later to the state police that when I came through the truck's windshield there was no sound anywhere in the world, and my arms were spread out like wings, my eyes open, and I was flying.

THE PRISONER AT THIRTY-SIX

There had once been a moment of what felt like synchronicity—
the doorbell of Janelle's walk-up ringing, a character on the TV
looking off-screen, as if in response—and from that moment,
that kernel, she constructed a world, one in which she too was a
character, her life an act, and after that it was easy—work, men,
family—because she always had the muscles in her neck tensed,
her head ready to turn to a sound from another world, her eyes
for an instant of recognition catching a woman alone on her
couch with a glass of wine, holding it a certain way because she'd
seen someone do it that way on TV once, and it just felt so right.

THE SHEEP YOU SHEAR WILL TURN OUT TO HAVE BEEN KOALA BEARS ALL ALONG, OR, HOW TO WRITE A NOVEL

1.) For no reason at all, Jenner is paranoid that one of his chickens is carrying an egg that, if hatched, could resemble him.

2.) Lexy lives at the corner and, if left alone in a closet, can open a bottle of beer with the back of her knee.

3.) Davis wears glasses he found on the side of the road. A dead lady had them half on. Nobody had found her then. Now he can't see without them.

4.) Where a speck of meteor falls, a mushroom will grow, with a cap like an ear. For this reason, Carrie has always been tightlipped around mushrooms.

5.) One Friday night, Maxwell learned to drink the syrup of his father's dreams. His father woke blankfaced and went through the motions of pancakes, but in the living room. Nobody ate them.

6.)   With the dead lady's glasses, Davis claims to be able to see Lexy in the closet, but really he's seeing the last time she opened the beers, or the next. The shadowy outline of her skirt is different.

7.)   Carrie sometimes lures Lexy out to the woods to get her to tell secrets. Lexy just whispers and whispers, and never looks at the ground by her feet.

8.)   Maxwell's father and Maxwell's mother wrecked off the side of the road one night. Maxwell's father walked in a daze through the woods until the deputies found him. Davis's mom had a bird sitting on her face when they found her. And no glasses.

9.)   The only love note Carrie's written so far, she left a line at the top for the name to go. Because she wants to be ready. Some of the X's and O's at the bottom of the page have been erased, then written in again, then erased again.

10.)   The back of Lexy's knee is ridged with scars, like letters all written in one place. All the secrets she knows have to do with Jenner, who lives next door. She sometimes sees him scurrying.

11.)   Pancakes occasionally show up on the floor of the attic over Maxwell's living room. Before they can cool, the raccoons are on them. They have hands like people and masks like people but they don't know regret, so are just animals.

12.)   For show and tell, Jenner brings his favorite chicken to class. When Davis walks in he looks into the chicken from the side and then up into Jenner, studying the line of his jaw, and then he looks as far away as he can for the rest of class. Carrie writes his name on a line and then cups her hand over it, to keep it there.

THE GIRL WHO KEPT KILLING PEOPLE WHEN THEY CAME TO HER HOUSE

Finally they stopped coming over.

GREEN PANTS

The time I tried to ride one of Tim Lawson's roller skates down the front steps of his house and he led me back to my house with my teeth pushing through my cheek for my father to drive me to the hospital, I don't remember the pain so much or the sun on my molars or that I didn't have to wear my seat belt this time even though we were running all the lights or my father watching me as he drove, but the parking lot where he pulled part of the way into an ambulance slot and crammed the emergency brake in. He looked over at me.

"You ready?" he said, and I nodded, and we opened our doors together, but I made it to the back of the car first because my father was standing in the privacy of his still-open door taking off his pants. I just looked at him, the blood collecting in the hollow of my collarbone.

My father smiled.

"New pants," he whispered, nodding to the hospital, "they've got closets full of them in there," and then he took my hand and together we walked towards the emergency room, one of us with two kinds of smiles on his face—each with teeth pushing through—the other in his Sunday boxers, the ones with cartoon fathers and sons all over them, which are really the only kind.

WHY I WRITE

I write because I can't draw. I write because I can't cut to the basket slick enough to go pro. I write because I eat too many sixlets and drink too much tea and my fingers get all jittery, and I have to put them somewhere. I write because, for a few pages at a time, I can make the world make sense. I write so I don't end up trolling distant neighborhoods for pets. Not to pet. And not only pets. I write because a lot of what I read disappoints me. I write because a lot of what I read intimidates me. I write because I'm jealous. I write because I'll drive my wife out of the house if I have to follow her around, tell her all the stories in my head. I write because I think sometimes that I know the truth. Not to say it, but how it feels. I write because there's nothing more honest I can think of. I write because it's not work. I write because I want more toys. I write because I don't know what to say to people I know and love in prison. But I can send them books. I write because I love rollercoasters. I don't write because I want to live forever. I write because I want to live now. I write because a teacher once read one of my pages, looked at me like maybe. I write because all the rest of the teachers didn't even look at my pages before deciding about me. I write for revenge. I write because books are legal, and other things aren't. I write because I can't sing like Bonnie Tyler. I write because writing matters. I write because if I don't, I get trapped counting and cutting and cutting and counting. I write because when I'm not writing, I go out and do things that land me in the emergency room. Because I want the world to feel like it should, like it does on the page. I write because I can't learn to play harmonica. I write because books have saved my life. I write because I'm petty. I write because lying is the best thing ever. I write because I hate to be lied to. I write because I sometimes feel like I have too many secrets, too many almosts. I write because I don't know what to do at dinner parties other than go inside my head, where it's safe. I write because I've always been standing in the corner, even when I'm not. I write to scare people. I write to make people laugh. I write to let people cry. I write to hide. I write to see what I'm thinking. I write because the stories are coming out one way or another. I write because once upon a time I read the exact perfect book, and it changed me forever. I write because fiction is magic. You can reach across centuries to another person with it. Across galaxies. I write because my kids might not ever really know me the right way if I don't. I write because I'm always afraid I'm about to die, because I always wake expecting to die and trying to do jittery little finger combinations to ward it off. I write because I might luck on to something nobody else has ever even tried before. I write because I want so badly to just go the party, please. I write because if I don't, then I can't think of what else to try to do. People always ask me this, why I write. And it never makes the right kind of sense, that question. So I just stand there kind of squinting, looking around for when I can leave. Then they ask what inspires me. This makes a bit more sense, but not really. I'm never inspired. I'm always inspired. Inspire is the wrong word. I'm compelled. There are stories out there. There are stories in here. And I'm going as fast as I can, trying to trap them on a page in a way that they can still be alive. People sometimes write me and call me and tell me that this story I made up, I didn't make it up at all. It's their story. But it was mine too, for a little bit. I write because one life isn't long enough. I write because I lost all my action figures long ago. The game went on, though. The game never stopped.

BESTIARY

A BIOGRAPHY

I grew up in a land shaped by animals. The first bird I shot, I shot in a buffalo wallow. There would be countless more—owls and ducks, flying away with my pellet gun pellets lodged in them, doves I wouldn't learn to clean and eat for years, the blood on their yellow breasts like a dab of jelly on butter toast. Quail that were beautiful and pliant in my hand, scissortails that fell in looping arcs, their tails disappointing up close. Mounds of red and white and black woodpeckers my grandmother would point out for me, that, even with their bodies full of birdshot, still needed to be chased down in the tall grass. Once, on accident, a mockingbird that wanted to put me in jail, take away my gun. The hole I dug to hide it in was deep. There would be more. A bullbat, just to see if I could. A compact little hawk of a kind I've never seen again. I buried it too, then took three steps away, found a pair of rattle-snakes mating, and watched them until they saw me and tried to break apart, couldn't. Hours later, skinless, headless, no guts, they still rose from the pan of grease I was cooking them in, struck at me with their blunt necks. Another time I walked onto a pair of sand rattlers, never knew how purple and pink their belly skin was until they were dead. That same year a normal rattler pulled at my pantsleg but couldn't get through. I killed it for so long that the venom got in my arm, swelled it from wrist to elbow. Days after that, just to see if it was a thing I could do, or to see if it was something I shouldn't do, maybe, I got down on my knees before a rattler and we stared at each other for half an hour, until it started striking, so I had to time my ball-peen hammer perfect. I buried that snake in a deep, deep hole with an owl I'd killed that same day, then, to keep them there, upended a fifty-five gallon drum, drove it down around the owl and the snake until it was level with the ground, told myself it was over, now—me, them. That I was sorry and it was over. I was wrong. Later that year I would stand in the brake lights of a pickup truck and help beat rabbits' heads against the bumper, because they weren't dead enough yet, then throw them into the pile already spilling over the bed rails. Because it was summer, we couldn't eat the rabbits, had to throw them into a pit for the coyotes. Later, in the snow, with slide action rifles that felt so much like the air-pumps on my pellet guns, I would run down elk and mule deer and whitetail, and I would look though my scope one afternoon at what should have been a cow moose thirty yards out, broadside, but instead stood into a cinnamon grizzly, her two cubs tumbling into view. That time, my uncle guided the barrel of my gun down for me, and kept it there, and I looked over the top of my scope at that mother bear and wondered where my uncle had been three years ago in my buffalo wallow, when, out of birds but not daylight, I'd aimed for too long straight up, into a power line, and hit it, then felt the small slug immediately in the ground by my left foot, instead of the bones of my face. I dug the slug out. It was shaped like a mushroom, still hugging the power line, and I did any of a thousand things with it then, I suppose. None of them right.

ACKNOWLEDGMENTS

Grateful acknowledgment is made to the editors of the following publications where versions of these stories first appeared: *32 Poems, Air/Light, American Literary Review, Automata Review, The Big Click, Big Muddy, Colored Chalk, Conjunctions, Cutbank, Everyday Genius, Fiction Attic, First Stop, F(r)iction, Grasslimb, Hobart, Lightspeed, Literal Latté, Menacing Hedge, Microfiction Monday, Mississippi Review, New Orleans Review, New Texas, On The Bus, Passages North, Platte Valley Review, Quarterly West, Shadowbox, Southeast Review, SpringGun, Staccato Fiction, Stymie, Texas Highways, Third Coast, Trop, Tuesday Shorts, Vincent Brothers Review, Word Riot,* and *Yellow Medicine Review.*

The following stories are previously uncollected:

"Bestiary"
"The Boy Who Cried About Wolves"
"How to Know You're a Killer"
"The Joneses"
"The Lepidopterists"
"The Real Batman Story"
"So This Is What It's Like"
"Truth Is a Bearded Lady"

ACKNOWLEDGMENTS

"The Umbrella Tree"
"Why I Write"

The following stories are original to this volume:

"Another Night, Another Death"
"A Footnote on Tickling"
"Foreign Currency"
"The Girl Who Kept Killing People When They Came to Her
     House"
"Kiss the Chef"
"Leftovers"
"Spear Father"
"The Two-Wolf Life"
"Thirsty"
"Where We Live"

ABOUT THE AUTHOR

Stephen Graham Jones is the *New York Times*-bestselling author of more than forty novels, collections, novellas, and comic books, including *The Only Good Indians* and the Indian Lake Trilogy. Jones received a National Endowment for the Arts fellowship and has won honors ranging from the Mark Twain American Voice in Literature Award to the Bram Stoker Award. Jones lives and teaches in Boulder, Colorado. Visit his website at stephengrahamjones.com.

STEPHEN GRAHAM JONES

FROM OPEN ROAD MEDIA

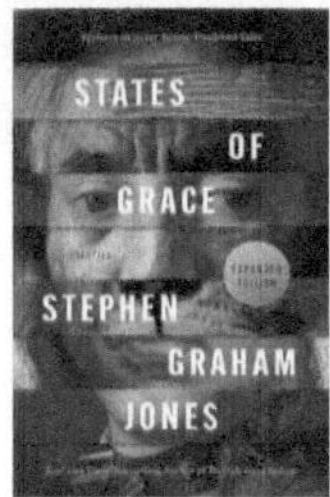

Find a full list of our authors and
titles at www.openroadmedia.com

FOLLOW US
@OpenRoadMedia

EARLY BIRD BOOKS

FRESH DEALS, DELIVERED DAILY

Love to read?
Love great sales?

Get fantastic deals on bestselling ebooks delivered to your inbox every day!

Sign up today at
earlybirdbooks.com/book